*Twelve m...*
*Twelve ind...*
*One UNIFORM...*

Don't miss Harlequin Blaze's first 12-book
continuity series, featuring irresistible soldiers
from all branches of the armed forces.

Watch for:

**LETTERS FROM HOME by Rhonda Nelson**
*(Army Rangers—June 2009)*

**THE SOLDIER by Rhonda Nelson**
*(Special Forces—July 2009)*

**STORM WATCH by Jill Shalvis**
*(National Guard—August 2009)*

**HER LAST LINE OF DEFENSE by Marie Donovan**
*(Green Berets—September 2009)*

**RIPPED! by Jennifer LaBrecque**
*(Paratrooper—October 2009)*

**SEALED AND DELIVERED by Jill Monroe**
*(Navy SEALs—November 2009)*

**CHRISTMAS MALE by Cara Summers**
*(Military Police—December 2009)*

*Uniformly Hot!*
*The Few. The Proud. The Sexy as Hell.*

Dear Reader,

Aren't these UNIFORMLY HOT! books an absolute treat? And the guys are phenomenal! They're honorable, loyal and committed to a cause greater than themselves. Add a touch of bad ass and voilà! You've got the perfect Harlequin Blaze hero.

When Special Forces officer Adam McPherson loses his right leg below the knee in a roadside bomb attack in Iraq, his world is shattered. But he's determined that his military career isn't going to be over. And since finding love probably is no longer in the cards for him, he figures hanging on to his job isn't too much to ask.

Thankfully, Winnie Cuthbert, who has always loved Adam, is ready, willing and able to show him that he doesn't have to lose anything, that he's still man enough to handle her.

I love to hear from my readers, so please visit my Web site—www.readRhondaNelson.com—or visit me at my group blog, www.soapboxqueens.com, with fellow authors and friends Jennifer LaBrecque and Vicki Lewis Thompson. We're always hosting some sort of party in our magical castle.

Happy reading!

Rhonda Nelson

# The Soldier

## RHONDA NELSON

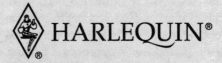

HARLEQUIN®

TORONTO • NEW YORK • LONDON
AMSTERDAM • PARIS • SYDNEY • HAMBURG
STOCKHOLM • ATHENS • TOKYO • MILAN • MADRID
PRAGUE • WARSAW • BUDAPEST • AUCKLAND

Recycling programs
for this product may
not exist in your area.

ISBN-13: 978-0-373-79485-0

THE SOLDIER

Copyright © 2009 by Rhonda Nelson.

All rights reserved. Except for use in any review, the reproduction or utilization of this work in whole or in part in any form by any electronic, mechanical or other means, now known or hereafter invented, including xerography, photocopying and recording, or in any information storage or retrieval system, is forbidden without the written permission of the publisher, Harlequin Enterprises Limited, 225 Duncan Mill Road, Don Mills, Ontario M3B 3K9, Canada.

This is a work of fiction. Names, characters, places and incidents are either the product of the author's imagination or are used fictitiously, and any resemblance to actual persons, living or dead, business establishments, events or locales is entirely coincidental.

This edition published by arrangement with Harlequin Books S.A.

® and TM are trademarks of the publisher. Trademarks indicated with ® are registered in the United States Patent and Trademark Office, the Canadian Trade Marks Office and in other countries.

www.eHarlequin.com

**Printed in U.S.A.**

# ABOUT THE AUTHOR

A Waldenbooks bestselling author, two-time RITA® Award nominee and *Romantic Times BOOKreviews* Reviewers' Choice nominee, Rhonda Nelson writes hot romantic comedy for Harlequin Blaze. In addition to a writing career she has a husband, two adorable kids, a black Lab and a beautiful bichon frise who dogs her every step. She and her family make their chaotic but happy home in a small town in northern Alabama.

## Books by Rhonda Nelson

This book is dedicated to our soldiers and their families, whose service and sacrifice are most humbly appreciated.

# 1

ADAM MCPHERSON HOVERED in that murky place between awareness and sleep, clinging desperately to the dream. He didn't know why it was so important, why he so fiercely resisted the pull of consciousness. But he knew when he awoke he'd be thrust unwillingly back into a very real nightmare and the dream…

Ah, the dream was so much nicer.

Soft womanly skin, greedy feminine muscles tightening around him, the delicious draw and drag between their joined bodies. Winnie's hot, lush mouth against his skin, sliding over his neck, her fingers in his hair. Her small foot moving up his right calf, eliciting a shiver as it brushed the sensitive skin behind his knee.

Adam gasped awake as the wonderful dream abruptly ended and the harsh unfair truth of his reality took its place. Though he knew his circumstances hadn't changed, he couldn't resist glancing down at his mangled leg just to confirm that part of it was truly missing.

It was.

In the time it took to process that fact, several other truths clicked into place, as well. First, his military career—or at least the high-octane kick-ass career he'd envisioned—could quite possibly be over. Second, despite the achingly perfect fantasy, Winnie Cuthbert could never be his. And third, the dream was a lie. Because he would never, ever be whole again.

Regret burned the back of his throat as he let the blanket fall once again into place. The panic he'd worked so hard to keep at bay suddenly reared up and threatened to pull him down again, back into that dismal place he'd found himself three and half months ago when he'd awoken from surgery and realized that something had gone terribly wrong.

While that godforsaken roadside bomb hadn't killed him, it had claimed a part of him he could never get back.

Though he knew he should be thankful—as far as the injury went, it could have been a helluva lot worse—it was hard to be appreciative when all Adam wanted was his old life back.

His old dreams. His old plans. His old body.

Three months in rehab—and counselling, of course, he thought darkly—at the Center For The Intrepid, a state of the art clinic for amputees and burn victims in San Antonio, and a shiny new top-of-the-line prosthetic later, he still hadn't quite been able to come to terms with his new circumstances. Oh, he put on a good show, though admittedly it had been harder when his brother, Levi, had been home.

Home for the moment being Bethel Bay, South Carolina, a sleepy little backwater town nestled just north of Hilton Head. Adam was currently staying at his parents' bayside home until his new orders came down. Orders that would ultimately decide his fate one way or the other. He'd either go back and do what he'd been trained to do, or be reassigned in some other capacity, still military, but only a shadow of the career he'd wanted and worked so hard for.

With Natalie Rowland-McPherson, his best friend and new sister-in-law, it had been easier to pretend that he was fine. She might have seen through him, but she'd never said a word. He smiled. Easy company, his Nat. He owed her a debt he didn't know that he'd ever be able to repay. Their playing cards, watching movies and generally talking trash had gotten him through the roughest part of being back home.

Levi, on the other hand, could look at him and read every worry, fear and self-pitying thought that he'd had since the accident. It was as awful as it was liberating. Thankfully, his brother hadn't tried to push him toward his so-called "emotional recovery."

He'd been content to simply hang out before leaving for his new assignment in Germany.

They were gone now—had been for two weeks—and the darkness Adam had managed to keep at bay for their sakes had descended with a vengeance. He knew that if he didn't manage to shake it off soon, he was going to be in serious trouble.

But this road, as arduous as it was going to be, was one he had to travel alone.

A soft knock sounded at his door, then his mother poked her head around the frame. Her hopeful expression made him wince. His recent decline hadn't gone unnoticed and the havoc it was wreaking on his mom's peace of mind made him feel like a selfish bastard. "Winnie's here," she said, smiling.

Shit. Again? Adam thought as every muscle in his body tensed. Why couldn't she just stay away? Didn't she know what she was doing to him? How hard it was for him to keep pushing her away when all he wanted to do was touch her, feel that smooth skin against his own?

After months of walking on eggshells around him, Adam didn't know why Winnie had suddenly decided to pretend like everything was normal—that he was normal—and started plaguing him to death as she always had. He gritted his teeth.

She was absolutely killing him.

Winnie Cuthbert had been right under his nose for the past ten years, a fellow athlete, partner in crime, peer and friend. And, though she'd always had a thing for him, he'd never been remotely attracted to her until she'd hugged him goodbye at his and Levi's going-away party. That simple, innocuous touch had sizzled through him like a blast from a lightning bolt. In that instant, as crazy as it sounded, Winnie had gone from simply being "a girl" to The Girl.

The one he had to have.

Even though he'd fantasized about her repeatedly while he was in Iraq, Adam had tried to tell himself that it was merely a fluke, that the almost indescribably potent attraction had to be a figment of his imagination.

Then he'd come home—damaged, shaken and unsure of everything else in his life—taken one look at her and had gone rock hard.

Hard evidence, indeed.

Given everything else that had happened to him, there was a measure of relief that had come with his affirming reaction, but regret had been quickly on its heels.

He didn't have time to want Winnie, anymore than he had time for the wallowing pit of self-pity he'd fallen into.

Adam had to focus on getting his career back.

Furthermore, Winnie wasn't some acquaintance on the fringes of his life, someone he could simply walk away from later.

She was a hometown girl with until-death-do-you-part dreams. And though the attraction was more than anything he'd ever experienced before, Adam's dreams were still firmly the same. None of them involved settling down in Bethel Bay. He was married to his career. And nothing—not even losing part of his leg—was going to change that.

Winnie was warm and funny, charming and loyal. She could bake like nobody's business, could shoot a basketball from half-court and catch only net. She had a wicked sense of humor and a pair of legs that made a man's mouth water at the thought of them wrapped around his waist. She could run a 5K barely winded and she was the only person who'd ever been able to get a hit off his slider. She enjoyed just about every sport—including football—and looked even better when she sweat.

In short, she would have been perfect for him, before the accident. If he'd been looking for something permanent. But he wasn't—then or now. All he could think about at the moment was getting back in the field, proving that it would take more than a roadside bomb to keep this soldier out of the game.

A niggle of something unpleasant, another protest

he didn't want to contemplate, hovered in the back of his mind, but he determinedly batted it away.

He didn't have time. That was the reason he didn't need to pursue this unholy attraction. Nothing more.

Additionally, though Adam knew Winnie genuinely cared for him, he still occasionally caught a flash of pity behind those dark blue eyes. And that was intolerable. His jaw clenched.

He would not be pitied.

Not by her. Not by anybody.

A fragment of the dream he'd had this morning surfaced once again, sending a fresh shard of longing through him. He bit back a groan. His loins caught fire, an altogether unpleasant sensation when his mother was still standing in the doorway, dammit.

"Tell her I'm in bed," he finally said, then he rolled over and pretended not to see the dejected look on his mom's face. Although, he did have to get out of bed sooner or later, Adam thought. Merely thinking about getting his career back sure as hell wasn't getting him any closer to that goal.

"If that's what you want," she finally murmured, a soft sigh of disappointment in her voice.

Adam resisted an ironic laugh. No, it wasn't what he wanted. What he wanted was standing at the front door, probably wearing something cute and sporty, a clear sheen of gloss on those distractingly gorgeous lips, her black curly hair in delightful, sexy disarray.

How in the hell had he missed that? Adam wondered again for what felt like the hundredth time. How had he not seen her? And why in God's name did he have to see her now?

As for what he wanted…

He wanted to reenact the dream he'd just had in the flesh, every single depraved scenario. And damn, how he wanted to kiss her, just feel the soft slide of those beautiful lips beneath his. Though he knew it wasn't entirely reasonable, he imagined that she'd taste like sugar, like one of those damned delectable cakes she'd continued to bring to him from her bakery. He didn't trust himself to look at her for any length of time without acting on this unrelenting need.

He couldn't. But damn how he wanted to.

He wanted to thread his fingers through hers and tug her to him, feel her lithe, warm body aligned with his. He wanted to breathe her in and eat her up. He wanted to slide in and out of her feminine heat until every unpleasant thought was banished permanently from his head. He wanted to take her until he died or his balls burst, whichever came first.

Adam chuckled darkly. Either scenario worked for him, so long as he could have her. He released a pent-up breath.

But he couldn't follow that road.

He'd sacrificed part of his leg for his career and he'd be damned before he let an injury take it away from him.

He was still a soldier, dammit.

# 2

"I'M SORRY, DEAR," Mrs. McPherson said when she returned to the door. "He asked me to tell you that he's still in bed."

Winnie Cuthbert felt her eyes widen. "But it's ten o'clock." Panic hit. "Did he have a bad night? Is something wrong?" Had the nightmares returned? she wondered. She knew Adam had suffered night terrors for the first few months after the accident, but she'd thought they'd stopped.

Mrs. McPherson's eyes were kind and guarded. "Not that I know of."

"Oh." A little punch of pain landed in Winnie's gut. So, he just didn't want company—her company, specifically. Winnie chewed the inside of her cheek, struggling to keep her goal in focus. This wasn't about her and what she wanted. This was about Adam and what was best for him.

And what Adam wanted more than anything in the world was to return to his Special Forces position in the US Army. Unfortunately, while he had been assured he would be able to return to active duty, whether he'd be able to return to Iraq, in his previous capacity, was still in question. In two weeks he would go through some sort of physical and mental evaluation which would determine that outcome. But instead of taking advantage of every minute to train and prepare, the idiot was still laying in bed.

At ten o'clock.

It would not do.

Winnie smiled determinedly. "Mrs. McPherson, do you mind if I go try to rouse Adam?"

Seemingly pleased, she opened the door wider. "I think that's an excellent idea, Winnie."

Winnie nodded once, lifted her chin and started toward Adam's room. The nerve of the man, she thought, fuming. Here she was trying to be noble and self-sacrificing—by helping Adam reclaim his dream she was essentially giving up hers—and he had the nerve to throw her efforts back in her face? Didn't the moron realize she was trying to be helpful? To love him enough to let him go, instead of rejoicing in the fact that he was finally home in Bethel Bay?

Rather than knock, Winnie simply opened the door and stepped inside. The sight of Adam's prone form nestled partly under the covers, his scarred thigh and what remained of his leg on top, momentarily shook her resolve. She'd seen it, of course, and couldn't begin to imagine the pain, the agony of the injury. Emotion clogged her throat and her heart rate kicked up a notch.

"Mom, I told you to tell her—"

"I'm not your mother. And if you're going to be rude, then you can damn well do it in person."

Adam jerked upright and immediately pulled his injured leg under the sheet. Her chest ached. As if she cared, Winnie thought. How could she look at him and not be grateful for the sacrifice he'd made? Did she mourn his leg? Regret that he'd lost it? Yes. But she was too thankful for his service, for his sacrifice to ever be anything other than humbled. Why couldn't he see that? Did he honestly think so little of her?

"Winnie?"

Ignoring his startled frown, she sidled forward and plopped lightly onto the side of his bed, forcing him to move over. His bare chest gleamed in the dim light, wreaking havoc with her senses and she caught a whiff of his cologne, something musky and warm. She swallowed a groan. This would be so much easier if she didn't ache for him so badly. If she hadn't dreamed of being in bed with Adam for more years than she was afraid to count.

It took every bit of strength Winnie possessed to ignore the fact that he was nearly naked and focus on the reason she was here. Adam had spiraled into a miserable funk since Natalie and Levi left two weeks ago.

It was time for him to snap out of it. And she had the difficult task of making that happen.

"Have I personally offended you?" she asked. "Done something to make you angry? Kicked your dog?"

He scowled at her, his wary eyes still heavy with sleep. "I don't have a dog."

"I didn't think so. So why are you avoiding me?"

Adam sighed and sank back against the headboard. A muscle worked in his angular jaw—the man had the most amazing bone structure she'd ever seen. It was criminally unfair. "I'm not avoiding you, Winnie."

Even his sideburns—bronze and a little longer than what was currently fashionable—were incredibly sexy. He was art personified. Living beauty. Simply perfect. Or at least to her, anyway. He always had been, damn him.

"You're not? Let's review the evidence, shall we? I've been by four times since Levi and Natalie left, at varying times of the day, and you're always sleeping. Either you're suffering from an undiagnosed case of narcolepsy, or you're avoiding me. I want to know why. We've been friends for years. Not as close as you and Natalie, I'll admit—" Though it wasn't easy. She'd always envied her friend that relationship. "—but close enough that you shouldn't be hiding behind your mother, cowering in your bedroom like I'm some sort of stalker."

His lips twisted into a shadow of his former grin, making her heart jump into an irregular rhythm. "And yet you're in my room."

"Because you won't come out of it. Since when are you such a coward?" she asked, purposely using the word because she knew it would needle him. Predictably, his expression blackened. "If you're angry with me, just say so. If you want me to stop trying to see you, then tell me why. It's not hard."

A dark chuckle rumbled up his throat, some inside joke apparently because she didn't see what was remotely funny. Winnie quirked a brow, waiting for an explanation.

He shifted and adjusted the comforter over his lap. "I'm not angry with you, Winnie," he said. Hearing her name come from his lips in that smooth southern baritone never failed to make her glow from the inside out. "I'm just trying to work through some things and it's easier—"

"—in bed?" she interjected. She was inclined to agree.

He laughed and that husky chuckle made her belly turn to goo. "No." His gaze tangled with hers, then dropped to her mouth. "Although that is an intriguing idea." He rubbed a line from between his brows. "What I was going to say is 'to do it alone.'"

She swallowed, resisting the urge to fan herself. The innuendo in his words had her thighs tingling. An intriguing idea indeed.

Still, having anticipated the crack-brained reasoning behind his self-imposed seclusion, Winnie was prepared with a defense.

Adam was hurt—suffering in a way she couldn't even begin to fathom. And, rather than inflict his pain on everyone around him, he preferred to withdraw into his cave and endure alone. No doubt he thought he was being noble and unselfish. She understood all of that. But his approach wasn't working—for him or anyone else. In fact, it was having the opposite effect. And every day he stayed holed up in his room was one more day that put him closer to giving up on the one thing she knew he couldn't bear to lose.

His career.

Unlike most of the boys she'd known in high school, Adam—and Levi, as well—had always been certain about what they'd wanted to do with their lives. With a father who'd been career military, a man who'd spoon-fed a love of country and a sense of duty into them from the time they were born, the brothers had always known that a life in the service would be for them, as well.

When asked where he wanted to go to college, Adam only had one answer: The Citadel. When questioned about which branch of the service he aspired to, he was just as brief: Army, Special Forces. He'd never wavered, had always been so certain of his course, of the path his life would take. She doubted that Adam had ever considered a contingency plan because there'd never been any other option. He set a goal, developed tunnel vision and saw it through.

She'd seen it time and time again, with everything he set his mind to, whether it was obtaining high marks in school or killing the competition on the playing field. His focus was unshakable. She'd often longed to have some of that formidable attention directed at her. A shuddering breath leaked out of her lungs as she imagined just what it would be like to be on the receiving end of Adam McPherson's unwavering attention. Having that heavy-lidded blue-green gaze locked onto hers, the merest touch of his fingertips beneath her jaw…

At the moment she just wished he wasn't so equally determined to avoid her.

She could help him, if he'd only let her. Though she hadn't wanted to revert to goading him into competition with her—her typical mode of operation in the past—Winnie didn't see any other way. The direct approach wasn't working. Thankfully, rather than being intimidated by her athleticism, Adam had always seemed to admire that trait, a fact that warmed her to no end. He appreciated a little friendly competition and didn't complain—or claim to have let her won—when she occasionally bested him at something.

Occasional was actually a stretch. She'd only beaten him once, at pool, so she wasn't even sure that counted.

Interestingly, where her tomboyish tendencies had turned off other guys, Adam seemed to appreciate her capabilities. She imagined that little quirk was what had made her fall in love with him to start with.

That…and so much more.

Though Winnie couldn't pinpoint the exact moment she'd lost her heart to Adam, the fact that he'd owned it for the majority of the past decade couldn't be denied. While she didn't strictly believe in love at first sight, she could distinctly remember the first time she'd seen Adam. And her reaction had been even more memorable.

She'd literally frozen in her homeroom desk, a violent full-body blush staining her from one end to the other. He'd greeted that flush of pleasurable heat with a small wondering smile and she'd known in that single, life-changing instant that he was going to be special to her.

But if her physical reaction to Adam had been

strong, then the emotional one had been almost inhumanly persuasive. It had rendered every guy who she'd ever dated—or would date in the future—pointless. It had fueled her dreams and shaped her fantasies. It had made her ecstatic and miserable, lifted her up and knocked her down.

It had defined her existence.

Identifying what made Adam the perfect man for her was impossible to put into words. His laughter made her want to sing. His character made her chest feel tight. Loyalty, integrity and honor were all inherent in his make up. He was the kind of guy who stopped to help little old ladies cross the street. He fought with the strong to defend the weak. He commanded respect in other men and inspired confidence—and awe—in women.

He was categorically good to the core. That's why she loved him, even though she knew he'd probably never love her back, never want the home and family she longed for. That's why she had to help him find his way back to his dream.

A lump rose in her throat as her gaze slid over him once more. Lines of fatigue were etched around those unusual blue-green eyes—the shade of a clear sea—and his perpetually smiling mouth seemed weary of the forced grin. Rather than keep the high and tight military hair style, Adam had let his messy bronze curls grow out over the past few months so that he more resembled the boy she'd known.

He'd always been particularly vain when it came to his hair—and with good reason. It was truly his crowning glory. He'd once told her that getting a military cut almost made him think twice about joining the Army. She doubted that, but she'd shed a few tears for those gorgeous curls all the same. Ridiculous, she thought now, to have cried over his hair when he'd sacrificed something so much more permanent.

"So…was there a reason you dropped by? Into my bedroom?" he asked, his lips sliding into a significant smile. A hum of electricity thrummed between them and she momentarily lost her breath. Funny, Winnie thought. She almost imagined that he could feel it, too. The way his gaze lingered along her throat…

Nah, she told herself. Wishful thinking. Just like the night he'd left last year when she could have sworn that she'd felt a change in the way his arms tightened around her. It was just a product of her ridiculous one-sided attraction. Besides, this was her opportunity.

Winnie blinked and tried to focus. "Actually, I was going to see if you could help me out. But don't worry about it." She waved a dismissive hand. "I can see that you're not up for it." She stood. "Maybe Mark Holbrook can—"

Adam grabbed her hand, jerked her back down

onto the bed with a speed that startled her. His eyebrows formed a hard line. "Shouldn't you ask me first before you get a replacement?"

His fingers twined unexpectedly through hers and the sensation was so bittersweet she struggled to focus. His hand was big and warm, calloused and curiously soft. It utterly engulfed hers and the sensation left her feeling protected. Safe.

She frowned, determined to play her role correctly as his thumb distractingly rubbed the inside of her wrist. "But you just said you'd rather be alone. I don't want to interfere—"

He sighed wearily. "What do you need, Winnie?"

You, she thought, her breasts tingling. Just you. Now. Here.

She swallowed the insane urge to laugh. "I'm coaching a girl's softball team—eleven and twelve year-olds. Unfortunately, my assistant coach pulled a muscle in her back during batting practice. There are three games left in the season and I could really use another pair of hands."

Because he was frighteningly intelligent—a brilliant strategist, from what she'd heard—he merely stared at her. "And there isn't a parent available?"

Winnie conjured a tragic sigh. "Clearly you've never navigated the political environment of girl's softball. If I ask a parent, then I'm going to be accused of playing favorites. It's just easier to get outside help." She shrugged, feigning unconcern, and started to stand again. "Seriously, it's not a big deal. I can ask someone else. Mark has been quite keen to—"

He pulled her down again, this time with a little more force, which sent her tumbling back onto him. Winnie landed against his chest, her lips a mere inch from the intriguing hollow of his collarbone. She was suddenly hit with the almost uncontrollable urge to lick that indentation, to taste his smooth, hot skin. Desire bolted through her, making her breath come too fast, her belly quiver. She gasped and her gaze slowly traveled along his neck, past the sharp angle of his masculine jaw. God, how she longed—literally ached—to trace his face with her fingers, to feel the rasp of stubble abrade her hands.

Her gaze finally bumped into his and the answering heat and confusion she saw there momentarily knocked the breath out of her. He blinked, dispelling the illusion, leaving her disoriented. Feeling a blush race to her hairline, she righted herself and, hands trembling, straightened her shirt.

"Mark Holbrook doesn't know one end of the bat from the other," he said, his voice irritated, but not altogether steady. "Surely you can do better than that."

Funny, Winnie thought. He almost looked… jealous. Another trick of her lust-ridden mind. He wouldn't be jealous on her account. He was only annoyed at the implied competition. She'd counted on that. It was the cornerstone of her goad-him-into-better-health plan.

Besides, Adam had always hated Mark Holbrook. Mark had an over-inflated opinion of his own intelligence, wit and skill. In truth, Mark was a self-important jackass, but Winnie wasn't above using Adam's intense dislike of Mark to her own advantage.

She arched a brow and glared at him. "I've been trying to get someone better," she said pointedly, her lips twisting into a smile. "But I'm not having much luck."

But from the speculative look in his eye, Winnie suspected her luck was about to change. She resisted the swell of hope that expanded in her chest, but couldn't quite fully tamp it down.

She released a small expectant breath. "So, what do you say, Coach? Will you help me?"

# 3

WILL YOU HELP ME? Four innocent little words and yet, irrationally, Adam felt like he was being cornered, forced into some sort of trap…like the almost irresistible one that lurked between her thighs. Something told him if he ever found himself there, he'd never want to leave.

But the idea of Mark Holbrook, the opportunistic bastard, taking his place was enough to set his teeth on edge. How could she even consider that muscle-bound gym-rat as a comparable replacement for Adam? Had she lost her mind? Was she purposely trying to make him lose his?

Probably, he thought broodingly…and it was working.

The merest notion of another guy coming to her rescue was about as palatable as a steaming plate of goose shit, and he couldn't stomach, either.

He slid her an appraising glance. "Do you really need my help or have you been given instructions to babysit me?" Natalie's "stop avoiding Winnie" comment the last time they'd talked came to mind, pricking his suspicions. It would be so like his friend to enlist Winnie's help in keeping him occupied. In keeping him sane and entertained. He knew both Levi and his new wife were worried about him.

Admittedly, Adam's mood had sort of taken a nosedive since they'd left, but this had been the first time since the accident that he'd actually been left alone, to try and sort out his thoughts. To grieve. The shrink at the Center had warned him of this possibility, but Adam didn't think he was truly in danger of becoming clinically depressed. He just wanted a little room to breathe.

His gaze slid over Winnie's smooth cheek. And breathing around Winnie Cuthbert was damned dangerous.

Especially right now. He watched her pulse flutter beneath her creamy skin and longed to taste that spot, to tug her back down against his chest. Her fingers were still entwined in his, soft but strong, and he had the oddest sensation of homecoming, of being anchored instead of drifting aimlessly.

He'd been drifting for months now and had to admit the grounded sensation was particularly nice.

Even if he had the time—which he did not—it would be beyond selfish to be with her, to encourage any sort of relationship at all. Even continuing their friendship, when he knew how much he wanted her and how she felt about him, was risky. She needed a guy who was going to keep a permanent address in Bethel Bay, not one who already had a foot—albeit a fake one—already out of town.

"I need help," Winnie insisted, but a guilty flush gave her away, signaling that her motives weren't entirely pure.

He waited, staring at her. Predictably, she caved.

Winnie rolled her eyes and released an annoyed breath. "And, of course, everybody's worried about you." She snorted. "Though I don't know where you'd get the idea that you'd need a babysitter." She smiled at him and a devilish twinkle lit her gaze. "You've got your mom to do that."

"Hey," he said, feigning offense. "That's uncalled for."

She shrugged, unrepentant. "You're the one who won't come out from behind her skirt."

"Knock it off, Winnie."

"Get out of bed, Adam."

He frowned, silently admitting that the reprimand was deserved. He did need to get out of bed. Particularly if she wasn't going to join him in it. Another flash of this morning's dream reeled through his mind, forcing him to shift the blanket once again. He glared at her, though it was hardly fierce. "You're annoying, you know that?"

A grin slid over her ripe lips. "You might have mentioned it…a few thousand times."

He speared his fingers through his hair and tugged, letting go a small groan. He gazed at her consideringly. "Exactly how much time is this going to take?" he asked.

Her eyes brightened. "Is that a yes?"

"It's a maybe," he corrected. "Time?"

"We've got practice today from three-thirty to five. I thought I'd work some drills with the fielders and you could handle batting practice."

"An hour an a half? That's all?"

"Well, that's all today," she qualified. "There'll be other practices and, of course, the games."

"Three games, right?" He wondered why he was stalling. He knew he was going to help her, if for no other reason than to keep Mark Holbrook out of the picture.

No doubt the scheming little monster knew that.

Truthfully, he did need to get out of the house, to show his father that he was up to resuming his post. Though retired, General Jack McPherson could still influence Adam's career. If his father saw that he was capable of returning to active duty, then Adam knew he would make an off-the-record recommendation, regardless of how his wife felt about it.

Sharon McPherson had made it exceedingly clear which path she wished Adam would take. Medic out. Come home. Do something else. She was billing it as an opportunity to pursue a different dream—a second chance. What she couldn't seem to grasp was that he'd never had a different dream. Being a soldier was the only thing he'd ever considered.

He was third-generation military. He'd been born to do this, to protect and defend. To serve. While other guys had been flipping through skin magazines—and he'd admit to taking the occasional peek as well—he'd been studying American history, reading biographies of past presidents and military leaders. He'd been absorbing military strategy, deconstructing every conflict in order to see what worked and what hadn't. His favorite game had been Risk and to this day, he'd never lost. He inwardly smiled. World domination had always been his M.O.

Being a soldier was more than a career choice—it was who he was. It had been hard-wired into his DNA, just as much a part of him as the skin on his body or the thoughts in his head.

He didn't know what else to be and didn't want to be anything else.

If he truly wanted that to happen, Winnie was right. He had to get out of bed.

And he had to stay the hell away from her.

Yes, he would help her with her softball team, but that would be the extent of it. She would see that he was making progress and report back to Natalie and Levi. Then she would have fulfilled her duty and could leave him alone.

The idea stung. Even now his body yearned for a deeper connection with her, longed to hold her hand again and so much more. Every cell in his body sang at her nearness. If she shifted the slightest little bit, he could feel himself adjusting, leaning toward her. He'd never been more attuned to a woman before, never wanted one with this sort of intensity.

It was a distraction he couldn't afford. But…

"Three games and a couple practices? Is that right?"

She nodded, her expression cautiously hopeful. "That's right."

"I'll do it on one condition," he said, knowing he was going to regret this. This was a slippery slope and he was already sliding.

She grinned, that adorable dimple winking in her left cheek. "Name it."

"I don't ever want to hear the name Mark Holbrook leave your lips again," he said darkly.

He'd be damned before he'd let the impressively

manipulative little minx play that card again. Scheming wench. When it came to strategy, she too was a force to be reckoned with. It was strangely attractive, he thought with reluctant admiration. A worthy opponent.

But this was no game.

He watched her fight a smile and lose. A twinkle lit that dark blue gaze and something flashed behind her eyes—satisfaction, maybe?—that he couldn't readily identify.

Unexpectedly, she bent forward and pressed a kiss to his cheek, making his dick jerk hard in response.

"I'll see you at the park at three-thirty," she said, then popped up and speedily left the room, completely unaware of the little bomb of desire she'd just dropped into his lap.

Not that he'd needed it. He'd had a perpetual hard-on since his dream and the damned thing had practically turned to granite when she plopped down on the side of his bed. He gritted his teeth, willing the unyielding erection away.

Shit, Adam thought. If he didn't get himself under control, playing ball was going to take on a whole new meaning.

"WHAT DO YOU THINK?" Jana Mulrooney asked, gesturing toward the drawing she'd brought into the bakery for Winnie's consideration. "Can you make a cake like this?"

"I can," Winnie said slowly. She released an uncertain breath. "But are you absolutely sure that you want me to?"

A hard laugh gurgled up Jana's throat and her light blue eyes were like chips of ice. "Eddie's balling his secretary, Winnie," she said. "I'm sure."

In her place, Winnie knew she'd undoubtedly feel the same, but Jana's plan seemed a little…extreme. Giving her cheating bastard of a husband a cake in the shape of a pile of dog doo with the message "Eat Shit and Die" on the top was perfectly reasonable in Winnie's book. But presenting it to him at his parents' fiftieth wedding anniversary party was bad form.

Especially when Winnie was making their anniversary cake, as well.

She grimaced. "I'll make the cake, Jana, but I think you should reconsider the timing," she tacked on gently.

For the first time, Jana's anger slipped and her eyes filled with tears. She choked on another bitter laugh. "Timing?" she parroted. "I'm pregnant, Winnie. How's that for timing?"

Winnie smothered a gasp and gave her old friend a sympathetic smile. "Oh, Jana, I don't know what to say." Ordinarily congratulations would be in order, but in light of everything else, she couldn't begin to imagine how Jana must feel. On second thought, yes she could. Her eyes narrowed.

She'd feel like killing him.

"Can I do anything?" Winnie asked softly.

Jana stuffed a Kleenex back into her purse and pushed her lips into a mangled smile. "Just make the cake—I know it's short notice—and I'll take care of the rest."

Winnie leaned against the counter. "Does he know?"

"No." Jana sighed. She looked out of the plate-glass windows, onto the streets of Bethel Bay and watched as people strolled along the quaint cobble-stoned walkways. "I was going to surprise him at the office and I'm the one who came away surprised." Her gaze turned inward, her voice flat. "They never heard me knock, never heard me open the door. I just stood there, too stunned to move, to say anything. It was like I was outside myself, watching from a different angle. I don't remember closing the door, or walking back to my car. I hurled right there in the parking lot." She looked at Winnie again. "This cake represents what I wish I'd said. How I wish I'd reacted." She shook her head. "I was just so stunned. I couldn't make sense of it, you know?"

"When did this happen?"

"Yesterday."

Wow. "What are you going to do?"

"Beyond making him wish he was dead, I don't know yet."

"Jana, I'm so sorry. Do you want the cake to taste like shit, too?" Winnie asked, more than willing to do her part now.

She laughed weakly. "That would be impossible. Everything you make is out of this world."

Pleased at the compliment, Winnie tucked a strand of hair behind her ear. "Thank you. I try."

And it was true. She was constantly testing new techniques, new recipes and ingredients to make sure that her confections tasted as good as they looked. Otherwise, what was the point?

Odd how some things just fell into place. She remembered helping her grandmother make a gingerbread house when she'd been just a kid. The first time she held an icing bag in her hand, she knew she'd found her calling. She loved baking. Loved the scent of almond icing and sugar, the smell of fresh bread in the oven. And there was nothing more beautiful than a perfect wedding cake. Fondant, dragees and pearl dust were the favorite tools of her trade.

Thankfully she'd always had a healthy metabolism and a keen interest in sports to help counteract the extra calories she consumed on a daily basis. She glanced around her bakery, her little home away from home, and couldn't deny the pride and satisfaction she felt fill her chest.

This little shop had been a dream come true and she'd put as much time and effort into the aesthetics as she had the food she offered here. With varying shades of lavender, lots of silver paint and gilt, delicate lacy chairs and a black-and-white harlequin pattern on the floor, the small dining room's whimsical décor was reminiscent of Alice In Wonderland. She hosted tea, bridal and birthday parties and knew that those frequently booked events were a direct result of the atmosphere she'd created. She was proud of the life she'd made here, even if, admittedly, there were times she was lonely.

But only lonely for Adam.

Winnie assured Jana she'd have the cake ready for tomorrow, then watched her brokenhearted friend leave the shop. Honestly, the idea that Eddie was cheating made her absolutely heartsick. He and Jana had been high school sweethearts. They'd survived the college transition, the usual newlywed chaos, and had been trying to have a baby for almost two years now.

Jana had confided that the strain of infertility was wreaking havoc on their relationship. Still, Winnie would never have imagined that Eddie would abandon fidelity and betray Jana's trust like that.

That was one of the benefits to being single,

Winnie thought with a sad smile. She never had to worry about anyone cheating on her.

She paused, giving the thought more consideration, then shook her head. If she were ever to win Adam's heart, she knew he'd be faithful. She couldn't imagine Adam ever saying 'I do' and then reneging on those vows. It would totally go against his character, completely out of the realm of his abilities.

General Jack McPherson had taught both of his boys that a man was only as good as his word and they'd taken the lesson to heart. Don't say it unless you mean it, don't commit unless you're prepared to follow through. How many times had she heard those words come out of Adam's mouth? She laughed softly. Too many to count.

No, the woman who finally landed Adam McPherson would never have to worry about being lied to or agonize over when or if he was coming home. Adam was a rock, solid and immovable in his beliefs. Whoever eventually ended up with him would have a guy she could genuinely depend on.

If only that it could be her, Winnie thought morosely. If only he'd choose her, then decide to stay in Bethel Bay and build a life with her. Make love and babies and institute movie nights, hold hands and snuggle on the couch. Unbidden an image of a bronze-haired baby boy with heavily-lashed blue-green eyes suddenly materialized in her mind's eye, startling a soft gasp out of her lungs. Her insides twisted with sharp longing and her arms suddenly ached for that child.

Stop it, Winnie told herself, slamming the door on that line of thinking before it could do more damage. Just stop. This baby—their baby—was never meant to be.

Frankly, Adam had never intimated that he even wanted a family. It was career first. Everything else was secondary.

But God, how she wanted that life. How she wanted Adam…and knew that she would always want him. He was the disease and the cure, the poison and the antidote. Changing how she felt about him was out of the question. She'd tried many, many times over the years, but the end result was always the same.

She was incapable of not loving him…and therefore incapable of doing anything that would result in his overall unhappiness.

That didn't mean she didn't occasionally want to throttle him, Winnie thought, smiling. She did. And the urge to give him a swift kick when the blockhead did something stupid was almost impossible to suppress. Like staying in bed for two weeks. Idiot. He knew better. How was he supposed to rejoin his Special Forces team if he didn't rebuild his strength?

Honestly, if he lost his career, Winnie wasn't altogether sure how he would cope. He might fall further into a depression, but Winnie knew that would be just the tip of the iceberg. She winced.

In losing his career, he'd lose himself.

And she'd rather let him go again than let that happen.

Natalie thought she was crazy, of course, and wanted her to take the "seize the moment" advice she'd once given Natalie. But despite all the bravado, Winnie knew she couldn't do it.

In the first place, she lacked the nerve, sad but true. And in the second…she couldn't risk the rejection. Somehow it was easier to pine away for him without making a play than to share her feelings and have them rejected. She shook her head. After all, she still had some hope in this sad little scenario that a rebuff would completely obliterate. She'd rather live alone with the hope than alone without it. This morning, she'd accused Adam of being a coward, but in truth she was the one who was afraid.

She hated that, of course. In many ways, Winnie was a lot like Adam. She set a goal and saw it through. Sports, marathons, college and her shop were all prime examples of her tenacity. She prided herself on those successes. But when it came to Adam… For whatever reason, all of that courage and determination simply fell by the wayside. It melted under the heat of that clear blue-green stare, was swept away by the mere upswing of his smile. He was her one failure, her one weakness.

Her Achilles' heel.

Winnie glanced at the clock. Three twenty-five. It was almost time to meet him, she thought. And she was going to need every ounce of strength she had.

## 4

HE SHOULD HAVE WORN sweats, Adam thought, feeling the heat as every pair of eyes in the park lingered on him while he worked with the girls. But it was ninety freakin' degrees and the humidity made it feel like one-hundred. He had no intention of frying out here just to make everyone else feel more comfortable. Honestly, didn't they know it was rude to stare?

Manners, people. Here's a thought. Why don't you get some?

He gritted his teeth, and continued with batting practice, instructing one of the girls to stand closer to the plate and choke up on the bat. Who would have guessed that it would be easier for him to adjust to the prosthetic than it was for him to get used to the blatant staring. Most people were merely curious, others pitying. He was an anomaly to them, he knew, but it still didn't make it any less unnerving.

"They can't help it, you know," the tween on the

plate said in a low, matter-of-fact voice. Mallory, if memory served. "You're different. They have to look."

Startled at her candor, Adam blinked and then grunted because he didn't know what to say.

"I get it all the time, too. Because of my eyes," she explained. "You won't get used to it, but you'll stop caring." She said it with such authority he was irrationally inclined to believe her.

Her eyes? Ah, Adam thought, noticing the difference between the two for the first time. One blue, one green. There was a medical term for that, but he couldn't remember it.

"I used to wear colored contacts, but they irritated my eyes," she said. "Besides, I was only doing it to fit in and I'm not meant to fit in." She winked. "I'm meant to stand out. You are, too, now, so you might as well accept it."

Her blasé wisdom jolted a laugh from his throat. "How do you know I haven't?"

She rolled her beautiful, unique mismatched eyes as though it were completely obvious. "I can hear you grinding your teeth. You're going to give yourself a headache." She dropped an appraising look at his prosthetic. "How does that thing work? You don't even limp."

Adam noticed the pack of girls move in closer, evidently curious as to his reply.

"Beyond the fact that it's got hundreds of little sensors which adjust and react according to my weight and movement, I'm not sure."

He'd gone to half a dozen fittings to get it just right. He'd even been trained to cover minor repairs, and actually kept parts with him. But really, he was just extremely grateful to be vertical again. He felt completely helpless when he wasn't wearing it and, for a guy who'd never known an instant of insecurity, that had been a damned difficult adjustment. The evenings were still the toughest, when he took it off to go to bed. He was at his most vulnerable then and he knew it. It was…unsettling.

"You mean like nerves?" Mallory asked.

"Simulated nerves, I suppose," he said, nodding. These kids were smarter than he anticipated. Not that he had a terrible amount of experience with kids at all. They were an alien species, one he'd never given much thought to, if he were perfectly honest. Though he knew it pained his mother, he'd always been so focused on his career he'd never stopped to think about adding a wife and family to his life.

A sudden image of Winnie holding a bronze-haired baby with her dark blue eyes suddenly flashed through his mind, momentarily startling the breath out of him. Longing and a strange sort of regret welled up inside of him, both emotions so foreign and unexpected they shook him to the core. Adam mentally swore. What the hell was wrong with him? He'd never longed for that life? And regret? How could he regret something he'd never wanted?

Never?

Career first. Being a soldier, that's what really mattered.

"Doesn't it rub your leg raw?" another girl asked, thankfully pulling his thoughts away from that distracting, wholly unexpected line of thought. "I had a cast that did that once."

The group had drifted closer and was hanging onto his every word. "It did in the beginning," he admitted. "But I've got a special 'sock' that prevents that from happening now." He tugged a bit from the top and showed them.

"Cool," Mallory said, nodding as though she were impressed. "Coach Winnie says you can still run. That you can do everything you used to be able to do before your accident. Is that true?"

Winnie and her group had finished up and were strolling toward him. She'd obviously caught the tail end of the question because she merely smiled and lifted her slim shoulders in a small shrug. She wore a baby blue sleeveless T-shirt, a pair of gray shorts—which showcased an exceptionally fine ass—and socks with little pink pom-poms on the back. He inwardly laughed, wondering why he found that small distinction so appropriate and sexy as hell. Her tanned skin was flushed and dewy with exertion and it didn't take much imagination at all to envision her having the same look after a vigorous bit of hot, hard, sweaty bed sport.

She excelled at all sports, so he had no doubt that she'd be every bit as enthusiastic and talented in the lovemaking department. Just the thought of it made his balls tighten in his shorts, sent a stirring sensation through his loins. His gaze lingered too long on her mouth, causing her to frown slightly. With effort, he forced his gaze away.

"It's true," Adam admitted. "But I'm not so sure I can do them as well as before."

"That's what practice is for, right?" Mallory said.

He chuckled, wishing it were so simple. "I suppose."

"Enough, girls," Winnie said, sparing him the rest of the Q&A. "Game tomorrow at five. We'll be here for batting practice at four, for those of you who are interested." They formed a huddle, stacked their hands on one another's, then belted out "Sand Gnats!" A second later, they scattered, leaving him alone with Winnie for the first time since he'd gotten to the park.

"Sand Gnats?" he said, grinning. "That's a bit humiliating."

She nudged him with her shoulder and the contact burned through him. "Hey, no knocking our name," she chided, smiling. "My little bugs have done well this season."

She had a lot of talent on her team, so he could certainly see why. And she was a damned fine coach. She had a wonderful, encouraging, nurturing rapport with her girls. No doubt she'd make one helluva mother, Adam thought, before he could stop himself.

Shit.

Wrong line of thinking. Unless there was an immaculate conception, Winnie would have to be in love with another guy to get pregnant. Because he knew Winnie wouldn't do it any other way. The irrational pain that accompanied that thought was enough to make his hands ball into fists.

"How well?" he made himself ask, purposely trying to distract himself. All the more reason he didn't need to be around her. The attraction alone was too much to contend with. Adding all these other bizarre feelings—ones he'd never entertained about anyone else—into the mix was seriously messing with his head.

He couldn't afford to lose focus. He had to keep it together.

She started gathering equipment and loading it into a giant duffle bag. "Seven and two."

He whistled low and bent to retrieve a ball, absently noting how natural the movement felt. He heard the solid clang of a metal bat hitting a ball and a dog barked in the distance. Typical ball field sounds. Comforting. "Nice," he told her, impressed. "Playoffs?"

Winnie straightened and hefted the bag over her shoulder. Frowning, he wrestled it away from her and slung it over his own. They slowly made their way across the grass toward the parking lot.

"It's probable," she said. "Although, it still depends on how well we do in these next few games." She glared at him, but something in the expression told him she was secretly pleased. "I could have carried that, you know. I do it all the time."

"I know you can, but you shouldn't have to." He scowled. "Where are these girls' fathers? They should be helping you out."

She grinned and a sparkle of something he couldn't readily identify lit her gaze. "They're at work. Seriously, I've made cakes that are heavier than that bag."

"You wouldn't happen to have one in your car now, would you? I'm hungry."

Another soft smile. God, he loved her mouth. Full, lush and rosy, it had the strangest effect on his ability to breathe.

"Sorry, no. But you're more than welcome to

come share my dinner. I've got a pot roast and vegetables simmering in the crock pot at home."

He quirked a brow, surprised. For whatever reason, he just assumed she'd eat out. "You bake all day at work, then cook again for yourself once you get home?"

Using the keyless remote, she unlocked the doors to her small SUV and lifted the hatch for him to stow the equipment. Various tennis shoes, goggles and a swim cap littered the cargo hold. "If I want to eat, I do."

Her eating habits forgotten, he frowned and picked up the goggles. "What's with these?"

"I swim."

He knew she swam—she'd been on the team in school. He just wasn't aware that she was still doing it. "Regularly?"

"A mile and a half every morning," she said as though it was nothing. She snatched the glasses from his hand and tossed them back into her car before closing the hatch. "So I guess that's regular."

Though he shouldn't have been surprised, Adam felt his eyes widen. "A mile and a half. Every morning?"

She shrugged as though it didn't signify. "It's a stress reliever. And it allows me to settle down before I go into work. I just get in my lane and go, you know? Everything else gets tuned out."

A spark of competition flared in his belly before he could completely snuff it out. It had been awhile since he'd been in the pool, but he knew exactly what she meant. He'd spent quite a bit of time in the pool for his Special Forces training, but other than the wake-boarding he'd done at the Center, hadn't been back in the water since. But he'd wanted to be. He'd even had a special finlike prosthetic for the activity.

Still, he found the fact that she was going, every morning, for a mile and a half was somehow…galling. Impressive, too, he'd admit, but…damn.

Meanwhile, he'd been in bed…

"It's easy on the joints and builds endurance. It's great exercise and I have to admit I've noticed the difference when I run. I'm not so easily winded."

She'd always been a runner, so that didn't come as any surprise. No doubt she was training for another marathon, Adam thought, feeling like a complete slacker. His cheeks burned.

Swimming was fabulous exercise, the kind that worked fast. He should have been in the pool every day he'd been home, should have been doing everything humanly possible to get his body back into prime form before his next physical, the one his entire future hinged on. But he hadn't. Adam inwardly swore again.

He was an idiot.

"What time does the pool open?" he asked, determined to be there in the morning.

"Six."

He nodded and pressed his lips together determinedly. "Is it usually crowded?"

She gave a speculative hum. "Not crowded, but full. There are a few regulars, of course. The bobbers. Me, Cindy Matthews, Mark Holbrook—"

"The bobbers?"

A sheepish smile curled her lips. "The older crowd. They don't exactly swim. They…sort of… bob around. So we call them the bobbers."

Adam laughed. "Winnie, I'm surprised at you. You should have more respect for your elders."

"I respect them until they decide to start hogging the lanes," she said. An endearing wrinkle wormed its way across her forehead. "Then I get annoyed."

"You know who annoys me? Mark Holbrook." Because he was a glutton for punishment and unable to help himself, Adam moved into her personal space. "I thought I told you never to mention his name again."

He had the pleasure of watching her pulse flutter wildly against her throat and she struggled to suppress a smile. "Sorry," she said. "It was an accident."

"An apology doesn't fix anything. But, just this once, I'll allow you to buy my forgiveness with a cupcake."

She grinned and that dimple he adored made another appearance, inexplicably pulling the breath out of his lungs. "Done." She quirked a brow. "Before or after the pot roast?"

He grimaced. "No pot roast for me. I've got to hit the sporting goods store." He slid a finger down her nose. "See you in the morning, okay?"

She nodded. "Sure."

"And Winnie…thanks." He gestured toward the ball field. "This was better than I expected. It's good of you to do this. Those girls are lucky."

She smiled and shook her head, shrugging the compliment off. "I'm the lucky one. They're a great group of kids."

She was right on both counts. He was lucky, too.

Lucky that she'd barged into his bedroom this morning and called him out. It would be so easy to be with her, Adam thought. So easy to back her up against her car and kiss her the way he wanted to—long and slow, deep and thorough. So easy to get so caught up in her and how she made him feel that he'd forget everything else.

Easy…but wrong.

He had to remember that.


WINNIE STARED AT Jana's special request cake and released a rueful giggle. Maybe she shouldn't have made it quite so…realistic. Then again, realism in a cake like this was crucial, if she wanted the message to translate. She shook her head and laughed again, then snagged a box from beneath the counter. Tension tightened her shoulders and fatigue from a long day weighted her limbs. A sharp rap on the front door of her shop startled her. Her gaze automatically shifted to the source of the noise and after a moment's hesitation, recognition hit and replaced the alarm.

Adam.

She frowned as she hurried forward to let him in. It was after nine o'clock. What was he doing out at this hour?

"I saw the light on," he explained at her questioning look. "Do you always work this late?" There was a note of censure in his voice she found oddly endearing.

Dressed in a pair of khaki shorts and a dark blue T-shirt, the driftwood pendant Natalie had given him—the Chinese symbol for courage—attached to his throat with a leather cord, Adam looked like every good beach boy should. Casual, but polished. The only off-note were the tennis shoes. In the past he would have been wearing flip-flops.

Longing knifed through her and she caught the scent of the ocean on him, warm, tangy and salty. He'd been to the beach, she surmised, unsurprised. He'd always loved the water. His hair was tousled and she suddenly found herself keenly aware of the intriguing beauty of his masculine throat. She loved the muscle play, the smooth skin along the side of his neck just below his ear. She wanted to lick that little patch of tanned flesh and sigh into his ear, thread her fingers through his hair and feel those wonderful lips moving masterfully over her own.

Her breath, his, commingled.

Just a kiss, she thought as the ache grew. Just a teensy little kiss and she could be happy. It would be enough. Truly. She could make herself be satisfied with that. Was it too much to ask, really?

A puzzled line emerged between his brows. "Winnie?"

She blinked. "Er…I do when I'm working on something special," she finally managed to admit, struggling to gather her thoughts. Adam McPherson had always been able to scatter them with ridiculous ease. "I, uh… I had a last-minute order come in this morning."

His expression soured, then he followed her around the counter. "People shouldn't wait so long to get their act together," he complained, still obviously outraged on her behalf. "You should have said no. It's not a difficult word, but it's one you seem to have trouble with. Here, say it with me. No."

Winnie pointed to the cake she was just about to box up and smiled. "I couldn't say no to this one."

Adam's eyes widened in horrified disbelief, then a bark of laughter erupted from his throat. "Eat shit and die? Seriously?"

She smiled. "Told you I couldn't refuse."

Still staring at the cake, he shook his head and passed a hand over his face. "That is truly revolting."

She felt her smile widen. "Excellent. It's shit. It's not supposed to be pretty."

An odd wariness tightened his eyes. "It's not actually made with…"

"No! No, of course not. It only looks like shit, you idiot." She whacked him. "It doesn't taste like it."

He shrugged, a sheepish smile shaping his sexy mouth. "I had to ask. It's awfully authentic looking. And combined with the message, well…"

Winnie retrieved a cupcake from the case and handed it to him. White cake, chocolate icing—his favorite. "Now we're square," she said.

He took a bite, sighed appreciatively and smiled. "You are damned good at this."

A blanket of warmth settled over her heart at the compliment. "Thank you."

He jerked his head toward the shit cake. "So who is that for?"

Winnie grimaced sadly. "I made it at Jana Mulrooney's request, but it's actually for Eddie."

It took him less than a second to figure out what

sort of circumstances would lead Jana to ask for a cake like this. She watched the knowledge dawn in his eyes. "Damn," Adam said. "Stupid fool. He needs his ass kicked up between his shoulder blades."

"I vote for his balls," Winnie said, her voice hardening.

"Who with?" Adam asked, naturally cutting straight to the heart of the matter.

"His secretary. How cliché, right?"

Adam swore again. "Is she certain?"

"She saw them herself." Winnie finished stowing the cake into the box, then turned to look at him. "And do you want to know the most tragic part?"

Looking thoroughly disgusted, he leaned a hip against her counter. "From the tone of your voice I probably don't, but tell me anyway."

"Jana's pregnant." She relayed how the couple had been trying to have a baby, and how news of the pregnancy had prompted Jana's office visit to start with.

A hot epithet slipped between his clenched teeth. "What the hell is he thinking?"

A hard smile touched her lips. "That's the problem. He's letting the wrong head do his thinking for him. He's ruined their relationship and for what? A quick lay?" She tidied the countertop and could hear the frustration leaking into her own voice. "I will never understand how that can happen. It's 'I do' until 'I don't'? Then what? What's the point of getting married? Of saying vows if they're ultimately meaningless?"

Adam merely stared at her and grunted in agreement.

This was a hot button for her and always would be. Her mother had nearly ruined her parents' marriage with an affair when she'd been in high school. How her father had found the strength to forgive his wife, Winnie would never know. She was grateful, of course. But at first had to admit that she'd thought him weak. It wasn't until she was much older that she could appreciate how very strong he had to be. Forgiveness took strength.

Frankly, she didn't know if she'd inherited that strength. But her parents were happy now, off in their RV touring America, one scenic drive at a time. She missed them terribly, of course, but this had been one of their dreams for many years. She suspected they'd weary of the travel soon enough and then return to Bethel Bay. Their little community was like that. People left, but invariably, they all came home at some point.

She was banking on that with Adam. She only hoped he wouldn't be bringing a wife in tow.

The simple thought made her flinch in agony. Adam loving someone else, kissing someone else, making love to someone else. And her, watching from the sidelines…

"Are you all right?" he asked, concerned. "You're a little green."

Winnie shrugged the unpleasant thought aside. "Yeah. Just got a little nauseated all of a sudden."

His eyes twinkled with grave humor. "You're not pregnant, too, are you?" he asked jokingly. He clearly meant it to be funny, but the smile quickly fled as though the idea was somehow repugnant to him.

She smiled grimly and looked away. "Er…no."

"What? Mark Holbrook hasn't convinced you to carry his love child yet?"

Winnie stilled. He was fishing. But why? He knew he'd always had her heart. He had to know. Hell, much to her embarrassment, it had been the worst kept secret in Bethel Bay.

Winnie cleared her throat and shot him a speculative glance, trying to figure out why he'd tossed his line into this particular conversational pond. "I believe you have to be in love to carry a love child." She paused deliberately and smiled. "Then again there's always birth control."

She had the pleasure of watching his gaze grow slightly irritated with the purposely vague comment. Humph. It might be good for him to wonder if she and Mark Holbrook had something casual going on.

They didn't, of course. Winnie was incapable of casual. She'd tried it a couple of times during college, when she'd felt pathetic for being one of the last remaining virgins in her senior class, but she'd genuinely regretted the decision.

Frankly, she'd gotten more pleasure from her massaging showerhead than she had in either episode with the so-called real thing. She'd squandered her virginity and shared her body for a stupid reason. Youth wasn't always what it was cracked up to be. Since then, she'd been celibate, hadn't so much as felt a thrill of desire for any man other than the one who was standing in front of her.

He'd ruined her. Absolutely ruined her.

Take your own advice, Natalie had said, exasperated with Winnie's reluctance. If he gets his way, he'll be leaving again. Go for it. You've got nothing to lose.

But Natalie was wrong.

If he rejected her—and she strongly suggested that he would—she'd lose hope. And it was the only thing she had left.

Adam's pale blue-green gaze dropped to her mouth and lingered and, for a fraction of a second she thought she saw the same longing reflected back at her. He blinked, grunted and stepped back, purposely furthering the distance between them. "Huh. Well, you'd better use some form of birth control if you're messing around with him. His gene pool is a little murky if you ask me."

Winnie didn't know why, but the warning irritated her. How dare he post a no-fishing sign where he refused to cast a line? "I'll keep that in mind. But it's not his gene pool that I'm interested in."

She wasn't interested in him at all. Still, Adam didn't need to know that.

His gaze narrowed again. "What's that supposed to mean?"

"Don't worry about it. Besides, what about you?" she abruptly interrupted, deflecting the topic away from herself. "I hope you're being equally careful with where you're sowing your seed."

He blinked, then chuckled as though embarrassed and passed a hand over his face. "My 'seed' is moldering in the barn," he said, smacking his thigh significantly. "I've sort of been out of commission, you know?"

Irrationally pleased, Winnie inclined her head. "What? None of those nurses offered to make sure you're enjoying a full recovery?"

He smiled at her again and a bit of a twinkle sparkled in his eyes. "Er…no. But thanks for asking."

A thought struck. "No lingering effects in that area, then?" She couldn't believe that they were having this conversation, that she'd essentially just asked him if his dick still worked. She smothered a chuckle. But…she was curious.

And she'd be more than happy to help him in that regard, too, if he needed it. Hell, she'd even buy a naughty nurse costume if that's what it took.

She was shameless. Positively shameless.

His eyes widened and he straightened a bit. "Jesus, Winnie."

She blushed. "It's cool," she said, purposely misunderstanding him because this was fun. A bit wicked and thrilling. "I'm sure that your tractor will be firing on all four cylinders soon. You can't rush things…"

He gritted his teeth and looked heavenward. "My tractor is fine. Everything's in perfect working order."

She frowned, enjoying this little game far more than she should. "But if you haven't sowed any seed, then how can you know that?"

He glared at her and a small smile tugged at the corners of his mouth, as though something about this conversation were ironic. "Trust me. I know."

She lifted her shoulders in a helpless shrug and merely smiled at him. "That's good, I guess."

He pressed his lips together. "Well, I think so."

Winnie turned and started tidying the counter. "A test run probably wouldn't be out of order, though. You know what they say about…unused f-farm equipment." The bad euphemisms were beginning to get to her. She stifled another giggle and marveled at the direction this conversation had taken.

Adam chuckled, then crossed his arms over his chest and shot her a speculative look. "You volunteering to take it out of the barn for me, Winnie?"

Her sex actually tingled at the thought. "Nah," she lied shakily. "My goal is to get you out of bed, remember?"

He sent another curiously thrilling glance in her direction. "Sex and beds aren't mutually exclusive, are they?"

Winnie felt the back of her neck grow warm. He was flirting with her.

Adam. Flirting. With her.

And this was not wishful thinking. Not this time. "Er…"

A bit of wicked clung to his smile. "Are you blushing?"

From one end to the other, including parts he couldn't see. "No," she lied again. She fanned herself. "It's just hot in here."

"I'm comfortable," he said easily.

The wretch, Winnie thought. What the hell was he playing at? He'd made it a point to avoid her for the first few months he was home. And now…he was flirting with her?

Seriously?

The hope she'd been clinging to for years suddenly seemed not altogether impossible. Her gaze slid to Adam.

If she was reading this correctly—and she didn't see how she could be wrong—then this new…development cast an entirely different meaning on his recent behavior. Had he been avoiding her because he didn't want to be attracted to her? Winnie wondered. Or was it something else? Something related to the accident? Or was it the same reason he'd always avoided any sort of romantic entanglement with someone local? Because he wasn't staying.

Probably a combination of all of the above, Winnie decided.

But ultimately…it didn't matter.

Because if he was flirting, then he was interested. Finally. Her competitive spirit rejoiced right along with her heart.

And he could stop being her one and only failure. Because, after all these years, Winnie was finally playing a game she had a shot at winning.

# 5

EDDIE MULROONEY WASN'T the only guy in Bethel Bay who needed his balls kicked up between his shoulder blades, Adam thought as he watched Winnie towel dry her hair.

He won that prize, as well.

What the hell was he doing here? Why couldn't he stay away from her? If he'd wanted to swim, he could have come after he'd known she was gone, right? But no…because he was apparently a masochist—and because he knew Mark Holbrook would be here—Adam had to come the minute the doors opened, just like Winnie did.

His plan to avoid her clearly wasn't working. Not anymore. Not since she'd brazenly walked into his bedroom yesterday morning. He'd been doing well up until that point, but now he knew enough to realize that the game had shifted and he was no longer completely in control. If he ever truly was, Adam thought, and that was questionable at this point.

Winnie wore a no-nonsense one-piece bathing suit that showcased her perfect figure and a satisfied smile that came with an excellent workout. Desire sizzled along his nerve endings as his gaze lingered over the gentle flare of her hip, the soft swell of her belly. Her breasts were full and lush and the way the wet material clung to her made Adam itch to peel it away and reveal the soft skin underneath. His dick stirred in his trunks and he turned his back, willing the damned erection away.

Unsuccessfully, of course.

Yesterday, he'd been determined to stay away from Winnie because he needed to focus on getting back into shape. When he went for his final physical the end of next week, he needed to be in top form.

He did not have time to mess around with Winnie.

Literally.

Even as late as last night, just before he'd walked into her shop, he'd renewed his determination to stay away from her. Eyes on the prize and all of that. He'd told himself that it wasn't fair to act on this unholy attraction when he knew how she felt about him, when he knew that, ultimately, nothing had changed. He would still leave at the earliest opportunity and there was no room in his life for a woman on a permanent basis.

Other reasons hovered like foggy shadows

around his mind, but he refused to acknowledge them, to let them into the light where he'd be forced to examine them.

Then he'd walked by her shop last night and the unreasonable irritation he'd had at seeing her at work so late had drawn him up short. The next thing he'd known, he was in her bakery, looking at a shit cake and enjoying one of her delectable cupcakes.

All of that had been harmless enough.

But then the talk had turned to her possible interest in Mark Holbrook—Adam shot the man in question a withering look—and from there, things had spiraled completely out of control.

Last night when she'd casually intimated her possible sexual interest in Mark Holbrook, the jealousy—the sheer magnitude of revulsion—he'd felt had just about leveled his soul. The idea of her with any man other than himself made him want to rip apart everything in sight, made him want to break things and scream. Bile rose in his throat and desperation razed his mind.

He was not accustomed to any of these feelings. Because he'd never felt them before. Adam had never been the jealous type. Frankly, he'd never had any reason. In the past if he'd wanted a girl, he'd simply taken her. Though Mark Holbrook admittedly got on his nerves, Adam had never truly considered the guy to be any competition. Adam inwardly smiled. How could it be a competition if he always won?

But in this case…he couldn't win. Not ultimately. Because he was leaving. And Winnie needed a guy who would give her forever.

Could he have her? In a heartbeat, he knew. For reasons he'd never understood, Winnie had always had a thing for him. Being around her had always made him feel…special. Made him aspire to be the man she thought he was.

And that man wouldn't toy with her, knowing that he had no intention of staying. He might have lost part of his leg, but he would not lose his career. He had to get back on active duty, if for no other reason than to prove to himself that he still could.

But he couldn't have Winnie.

It wasn't fair. To him or to her.

And maybe if he said it often enough, he'd begin to believe it.

Winnie strolled over and nodded toward his fin. "That's cool."

It had actually worked a lot better than he'd anticipated. The technology was seriously ingenious. "Yeah," Adam said, nodding. "It felt good in the water."

"I was watching. You looked good," Winnie said. "Every bit as strong as you always were."

Adam grimaced. "I don't know that I'd say that,

but I kept up with you, so I'm happy." He'd actually been a bit worried about that. Though he'd been in good shape before the accident and had the best resources for therapy over the past several months, his body had taken a beating. He thought he'd bounced back quite well. But thinking it and having it confirmed were two different things.

And Winnie wasn't your average opponent—she was extremely fit.

She was also…different this morning. More confident. He'd tipped his hand last night and she was reacting accordingly.

In other words, he was doomed.

Winnie snorted. "That's all that matters to you, isn't it? Beating me?"

Adam smiled at her. "It's a perk."

"I've beaten you before, you know," she said, finger combing her wet curls.

Adam smiled and sighed. "That game of pool? I can't believe you're still clinging to that."

She shrugged, then casually dusted a bead of water off his shoulder. Her touch sizzled through him and he had the pleasure of watching her breath stutter at the innocent contact.

"Hey, I'll take my victories where I can get them." Her eyes twinkled. "Isn't it funny how you've never had the courage to play me again?" She sighed dramatically. "Losing to me was such an unpleasant experience that you refuse to risk it happening again."

"It's not that I don't have the courage, Winnie," Adam said, feeling a dare coming on. Resist, resist, resist. "I just haven't had the opportunity. There's a difference."

She bit her lip to keep from smiling. "Really? That's the only reason?"

"Yes."

"But if the opportunity presented itself, you would play me? You'd chance losing…again?"

She was enjoying this entirely too much, Adam thought. And as much as he needed to stay away from her—as much as he needed to focus on training—he knew he'd have no choice but to pick up the gauntlet, if she decided to throw it down. He couldn't help himself.

Need was beginning to edge out reason.

Again.

He stood, purposely towering over her, as if it would do any good. She wasn't the least bit afraid of him. And she'd never been intimidated by a challenge. It was part of the reason he'd always liked her. But under the influence of this damned attraction, he was finding the quality annoyingly sexy as hell.

As if he needed another reason to burn for her.

"Yes," he said. "I would play you." He grinned. "And this time I would win."

She lifted her chin. "Are you willing to put your money where your mouth is?"

He'd rather put his mouth where hers was, but he nodded all the same. "Sure."

Winnie's lips curved with triumph. "Fine. Meet me at Clementine's after the ball game this afternoon. Winner picks up the dinner tab."

Adam grinned. She'd just turned this into a date. Definitely a worthy opponent. "If you're buying then I'm getting the most expensive thing on the menu."

She laughed and poked a finger against his chest, sending an unexpected bolt of heat directly to his groin. "Better be sure you don't forget your wallet. I'm planning on running up a bar tab."

He frowned. "You don't drink."

She dimpled. "No…but everyone else in there usually does."

Adam shook his head. "You are evil."

She batted her lashes at him. "It's part of my charm." She turned and started to walk away. "And remember to bring cash, not credit cards," she called without looking back. "You're going to need it."

What he needed was a brain transplant, Adam thought, unable to drag his gaze away from her delectable ass, the hypnotizing swing of her hips. What the hell was he doing? When had he enlisted for self-torture?

He snorted. Probably around the same time he realized he wanted her, Adam thought.

And being around her only made him want her more.

Easy to fix, but hard to follow through.

And, God help him, he was slowly losing the will to try.

"EIGHT BALL, RIGHT CORNER pocket," Winnie said as she carefully lined up her cue. She felt Adam's gaze on her ass and a little thrill whipped through her.

"Are you sure you can make that?" he taunted.

Winnie turned and smiled at him over her shoulder, then deliberately took the shot without looking. She heard the gratifying thump of the ball dropping into the pocket and her smile widened. "I'm certain."

Adam chewed the corner of his lip, but it didn't hide his impressed smile. "You've been practicing."

Winnie straightened. "A little."

Adam stowed his pool stick—the one he never got to use—and shot her a beleaguered glare. "You cleared the table, Winnie. You beat me last time as well, but at least then, I got to play."

Winnie took a chair at the nearest table and began to confidently peruse the menu. "I figured if I was going to hang on to my one and only victory, I'd better brush up on my skills."

Adam joined her, scraping the chair against the worn linoleum as he dragged it against the floor. "And how long have you been brushing up?"

She jerked her head toward the wall where various photos of her local championships were displayed. "A while."

Adam's eyes widened and he swore, then shot her an outraged look and laughed. "I've said it before, but it bears repeating. You are evil."

Winnie chuckled. "Not evil, Adam. Good. There's a difference."

He shrugged lazily, cocked his head and then took a swallow from his beer. "Like beds and sex, the two aren't mutually exclusive."

A little breath stuttered out of her lungs and her imagination instantly created a vision of the two of them having evil, wonderful sex in the car at McKinney Point. Ridiculous to still be holding on to that fantasy, but she couldn't seem to help herself. McKinney Point was the local make-out spot. Adam had hauled so many girls up there in high school that Winnie had actually painted him a parking sign and erected it herself. She'd agonized over those girls— the ones she'd desperately wanted to replace—and the envy still had an unpleasant grip on her heart.

Still, the thought of that old sign and the hours she'd put into it made her smile.

Adam shot her a look. "Oh, no. What are you grinning about?" he asked suspiciously.

She laughed. "Just thinking about your comment."

"About having sex somewhere besides a bed?"

Yes, she was thinking about having sex with him at McKinney Point, but she damned well wasn't about to share that. "No, just thinking about all the sex you've had in places other than a bed." With other people, while she grieved.

He blinked. "What?"

"McKinney Point?" she reminded him, arching a significant brow.

His gaze grew reflective and a slow smile slid over his lips. "Damn, I haven't been up there in years."

She rolled her eyes. "I've never been up there at all."

Surprise flashed in his expression. "You never went at all? But you dated," he said. "That band guy. Whatshisname—Chuck."

Winnie chewed the inside of her cheek. "I went to the prom with Chuck because he didn't mind that I was a jock and I didn't care that he had enough metal in his mouth to fuel a nuclear plant," she said. Her lips twisted. "We didn't actually date and we never made out at McKinney Point." She lifted her chin and sniffed. "You, however, were a regular up there, usually with a different girl every time."

His eyes twinkled with masculine pride. "I wasn't as bad as all that," he told her, though the self-satisfied smile he was wearing indicated he knew otherwise.

"Yes you were," she protested. "You were a regular man whore. For crying out loud, you had your own parking space reserved up there!"

"That was a joke. Damned Natalie."

Winnie chuckled and ducked her chin. "That wasn't Natalie, Sherlock. That was me."

His eyes widened. "You?"

"Yes, me," she said primly.

His gaze sparkled with admiration. "That was devious."

"Hey," she said, innocently. "I had plenty of time. I wasn't hanging out at McKinney Point."

"So you've never been?"

She shook her head, took a sip of her water. "Nope."

"That's a crying shame," he said, staring at her. His eyes darkened and bit of a challenge hung on to his smile.

It would be easy enough to rectify, if he was so inclined, Winnie thought. And from the way his gaze was lingering on her lips, he was thinking the exact same thing.

A thrill whipped through her. She might have been stumbling around in a one-sided attraction for more than a decade, but she'd made up ground pretty damned quickly.

He wanted her.

She could tell.

For all the effort Adam had put into avoiding her for the past several months, he suddenly didn't seem to be able to stay away. She didn't know what—if anything—had changed, but she was damned thankful for the new status quo.

Frankly, though he'd promised to help her with her team, she'd imagined that anything outside of the ball diamond was going to be a struggle. But then he'd barged into her shop last night, adorably outraged on her behalf, and then shown up again at the pool this morning, glaring ominously at Mark Holbrook. If he hadn't wanted to see her, he could have chosen a different time.

He hadn't.

He'd come when he knew she'd be there…with Mark.

Though she could hardly wrap her mind around it, Adam—as mind-boggling as it seemed—was jealous of Mark Holbrook.

Because of her.

Adam drew back and determinedly snagged a

menu, a bit of a forced smile on his lips. Ah, she thought, noting the abrupt switch in his body language. He was still fighting it. Still determined to stay the course.

But she was just as determined to make sure he careened right off of it. She was too close, closer than she'd ever been, to let this chance pass her by.

Winnie knew Adam would leave. His career was first. She got that. But, pathetic as this might be, she didn't mind playing second if it meant she could just kiss him, hold him to her for a little while.

It would be enough. It had to be.

"So I owe you a meal," he said, overly cheerful, as though he could change what he'd shown her. "What are you going to have?"

*You, at some point,* Winnie thought. What she wanted wasn't on the menu. She was staring at it. Every perfectly sculpted, magnificent inch of it. Her gaze traced the lean slope of his cheek, the smooth curve of his jaw and rested on his wickedly carnal mouth.

She'd dreamed of that mouth and all the things he could do with it. To her.

And she was going to see that dream to fruition before he left if it was the last damned thing she did.

# 6

SHE'D NEVER BEEN TO McKinney Point, Adam thought for what felt like the hundredth time since the night before. Honestly, he didn't know why Winnie's admission had stuck in his mind, but the fantasies her words had sparked in his own imagination—foggy windows, heavy breathing, naked skin—were nothing short of X-rated.

Even as early as this morning, when once again he'd forsaken common sense and met her at the pool—why the hell couldn't he stay away?—he'd been thinking about sitting in the car with the seats back, her thighs bracketing his, a little rock and roll playing from the radio.

And her.

Adam pushed through the screen door and made a beeline for the fridge. Honestly, he didn't know how much longer he could keep this up. Especially since Winnie was upping her game. Casual touches, a lingering look and, though she'd probably had the little habit for years, he'd suddenly become preoccupied with how often she sank her teeth into her bottom lip. It was distracting as hell. The sly slide of her gaze when she looked up at him from beneath those long lashes. He didn't know how much of it was actually deliberate on her part or how much his lust-ridden mind was twisting even the most innocent gesture.

But there had been nothing innocent about the kiss she'd pressed to his cheek last night when they'd left Clementine's. She'd gone up on her toes, grasped his forearm and had come dangerously close to actually kissing his mouth. Probably because he'd started to turn his head, but stopped himself just short.

Though Adam would like to think that he was simply that strong, that his determination to do the right thing was that formidable…he knew better.

There was an underlying fear—almost panic— that had prevented him from giving into the moment, one he couldn't explain and most certainly didn't understand. So he'd forced the unpleasant notion away and told himself again that the only reason he couldn't be with Winnie was because he was leaving. Because she deserved a permanent guy. Because he wanted his old life back.

All of which were true. But even he was beginning to recognize that he was protesting a little too much. Jeez Lord, what a friggin' mess. Why couldn't he simply stay away from her? Why did he keep putting himself purposely in her path? Why, after all these years, had she suddenly become so damned important to him?

"Colonel Marks called while you were at the pool this morning," his father said, interrupting his internal diatribe.

Adam drew up short and every sense went on point. Colonel Marks was the officer in charge of his next assignment. He'd ultimately be the one to determine whether or not Adam resumed his post or took a new one.

Adam stilled. "He did?"

"There's been a change of plans. Your review has been moved up to Friday."

Shock eddied through him. "This Friday?" A week sooner than the original appointment. Why the change? Or better still, what had changed? Adam didn't know what to make of it. Why would his hearing, for lack of a better term, have been moved?

His father merely nodded.

"Did he say why?" Adam asked, but it was a pointless question. If the General had known why, then he would have told him.

"No. He asked if you were ready and I said yes. I was certain that was the answer you would have wanted me to give him…and that's the answer I believe, as well."

Adam looked up, surprised and grateful for his father's affirmation. The General had been very careful to keep his opinions and emotions to himself since Adam had returned home. He had been encouraging, of course. Solicitous, even. But he hadn't given any indication whatsoever as to what path Adam should now tread. Frankly, though he was curious about his father's opinion, Adam was glad that his dad had kept it to himself.

Unlike his mother…who had been very vocal. "Stay here. Medic out. Start over."

She was doomed to disappointment. That wasn't his dream and never would be. Adam was a soldier. Nothing was ever going to change that. Not even Winnie, though admittedly for the first time in his life, he was tempted.

"Have you told Mom yet?"

The General winced. "No."

Adam stared down at the trendy new tile his parents had installed to replace the dated pale green linoleum. "She realizes that she's not going to change my mind, right?"

"She does," his father admitted. "But that's not going to keep her from trying. Cut her some slack, son. This has been very hard for her. She doesn't understand. She's not—"

"I know, Dad." Adam passed a hand over his face. "I understand her concern, but I can't change who I am to make her feel better. Not in this." He couldn't change for anybody. He might have lost part of his leg, but he was still the same man he'd been before the accident.

Liar, a little voice niggled, but he determinedly pushed it away.

He was the same. He still had the same dreams, dammit.

His father adjusted a magnet on the refrigerator. "She doesn't expect you to, really. She's just worried."

Adam looked up at his father. "And you're not?"

"No more than I ever was. You have always known your own mind, Adam. You know what you're doing. I'll admit I was a little concerned in the beginning, but this past week you've shown the determination that's always been a big part of your character." His father stared at him, his face calm and passive, as always, but curiously intense, as well. "I don't know what Winnie said to you, but whatever it was, you should thank her."

He should have known his father would connect those dots. The General rarely missed anything. And he was right. If Winnie hadn't barged into his bedroom and provoked him into getting out of bed, who knows what might have happened? He certainly wouldn't have been ready for this meeting at the end of the week, that's for damned sure.

The end of this week.

As anxious as he was to be back with his boys, he had to admit that the idea of leaving Winnie made his stomach knot with dread. No doubt the next time he saw her she'd be permanently attached to someone else. And, as much as that would be better for both of them, the mere thought of that had the same soul-shattering affect it always did.

Winnie…and someone else.

He swallowed tightly and looked away, suddenly feeling claustrophobic in their large kitchen. Adam nodded his thanks to his dad, then he turned and made his way back outside. He had no idea where he was going, but just knew that he couldn't be inside the house anymore. He needed to escape his father's perceptive gaze and didn't want to face the imminent fallout with his mother when she found out he'd be leaving even sooner. Hopefully, the General would deal with that, so Adam wouldn't have to. Frankly, he didn't want to spend his last week at home trying to justify his decision.

Because he was a glutton for punishment, he'd admit that he wanted to spend it with Winnie. He wanted to slide his thumb over that plump bottom lip, feel her skin beneath his palms. He wanted to taste her, feel her, breathe her in. He wanted to spend every single second with her, to take what he shouldn't because it couldn't last and wasn't fair to her. To either of them.

He wanted to thread her fingers through his, wanted to feel her sexy mouth against his neck, her moist breath in his ear, her hot body tightening around him. He wanted to watch her eyes melt for him.

God help him, he just wanted to be hers.

But he couldn't. And for whatever reason, the obvious reasons he'd been telling himself were no longer holding water. Something else was going on inside him, but he was too afraid to examine those parts too closely. God only knew what he would find. Intuition told him it damned sure wasn't anything he wanted to face.

Maybe cutting his time short in Bethel Bay would end up being a blessing in disguise, Adam thought. It was less time to be tempted. Less time to screw up.

This would be a good thing, Adam decided, desperately looking for a bright side to this suddenly bleak future—the one he knew he wanted. Winnie could move on, he would move on. Life would… suck. Be empty. But it would be better than giving her hope, making her wish something that wasn't meant to be.

Suddenly jumpy with excess energy, Adam decided a run was in order. He needed to do something and since having hot, depraved sex with Winnie was out of the question, a mad dash along his favorite trail in Magnolia Park would have to suffice. And in that sense, trail was actually a loose interpretation. More like a path off the beaten path, but the views over the bay and town were second to none. He'd seen a couple of birders up there over the past week, but other than that it was blissfully unpopulated. And frankly, he could use some alone time.

He was more than a quarter mile in when it happened. He'd been waiting for it, knew that it would at some point. He just wasn't prepared to have witnesses.

His cheeks flooded with heat. Embarrassment absolutely scorched every cell in his body.

His foot—ironically, the real one—tripped over a root and sent him sprawling. He caught the flash of a pink T-shirt on his way down—almost as though it were happening in slow motion—and it took less than a second to place it and the woman wearing it.

Winnie.

She was jogging toward him, but slowed as she

approached, seemingly unsure of what to do. No doubt she'd offer to help any other person up, but given his circumstances, she wasn't sure of the protocol. He knew this, even understood it, but it didn't make him hate it any less.

A litany of hot epithets raced through his head, blistering his mind. How he wished she hadn't seen him like this—weak and vulnerable.

"I'm fine, Winnie." He sighed wearily, before she could take another step closer. "I don't need your help."

Something changed in her expression, something unreadable, but determined nonetheless. She lifted her chin a mere fraction of an inch, then sidled toward him, a slow, triumphant smile on her ripe mouth.

Oh, hell, Adam thought, his gaze narrowing as she approached. His heart rate kicked up a notch and, despite his humiliating position, his dick stirred in anticipation.

"Good," she said. "Because I wasn't going to offer it. I have something else in mind."

Then, before he could come up with a response, she dropped to her knees, put both hands on his shoulders and shoved him back against the ground.

"Stop running from me, Adam," she said. "It's getting old."

He frowned and a surprised oomph sighed out of his mouth…and, to his utter shock and pleasure, it sailed directly into hers.

The ardent attack-kiss caught him completely off-guard, robbed him of restraint and his body reacted accordingly. Hungrily. Desperately. Her lips were soft as silk, tasted faintly of almond icing and were so achingly perfect against his that it damned near made him weep.

Kissing Winnie. Finally.

How could something he knew to be so wrong feel so damned right?

He was doomed, Adam thought, as he framed her face, testing the feel of her sleek skin beneath his palms. A shudder wracked through him. Chills raced down his spine.

Ah…heaven. The longing he'd been beating back for months suddenly snapped like a rubber band that had been stretched to the breaking point. He felt the ricochet—the backlash—give a vicious tug behind his navel.

Then, with a groan dredged from the farthest recesses of his soul, he deepened the kiss and admitted defeat.

WINNIE WASN'T A person to squander opportunity and, considering that Adam was stretched out on the ground at her feet only seconds ago, she'd decided to seize the moment and take what she wanted.

If he hadn't almost kissed her last night, Winnie wouldn't have had the courage to essentially jump him this morning, but he had—damn his resistance—and she'd gone home frustrated and more determined than ever to make him lose that almost unshakable control.

Besides, there was nothing like a kiss to make a man forget that he was embarrassed and she didn't want him to linger over the fact that he'd fallen in front of her. She'd known a single moment of blind panic, but the muttered curse under his breath had assured her that he was unharmed, that his pride was the only thing that had been wounded.

So she'd kissed him.

Finally!

It was a sad state of affairs that she'd had to resort to basically attacking him when he was down. But given the fact that his wonderful hands were sliding all over her body, he didn't seem to mind. Though he hadn't so much as hesitated when her mouth met his—gratifying, she might add—she'd realized that there'd been a moment of complete surrender, a moment she'd been waiting for her whole life.

He'd gone from merely kissing her back, to devouring her.

Winnie tangled her tongue around his and pushed her hands into his hair, kneaded his scalp. Her fingers brushed the soft skin behind his ear and the curious swelling of affection she felt for that little spot made her smile against his mouth.

She was miserably, hopelessly, irrevocably in love with this man.

Her nipples pearled under her sports bra and her blood moved sluggishly through her veins. Warmth pooled in her core, inspiring a steady throb in her loins that made her want to slip and slide all over him.

Preferably naked.

Given the hot hard length of him nudging determinedly against her navel, Adam wasn't averse to the idea, either. Though they were literally rolling on the ground, now covered with dirt and debris, Winnie didn't care. The only thing that mattered was Adam and what was happening between them. She shifted over him, straddling him, and the instant she felt him between her thighs a hot sigh of satisfaction oozed out of her lungs.

He flexed beneath her, shaped his hands possessively over her rump and gave a slight squeeze.

She gasped and warmth coated her folds.

With an agonized groan, Adam tore his mouth from hers, and promptly reversed their positions. He kissed her neck, nuzzled his nose beneath her ear. A chill ran through her and even her toes started twitching in anticipation.

"Winnie, do you have any idea what you're doing to me?"

Winnie slid a finger along his jaw. "You didn't want my help. This was the alternative."

He chuckled softly. "Your mind is a mysterious thing."

"Mine? Ha. You've always had better insight into my mind than I've ever had into yours." She released a shaky breath.

"Yours is more interesting."

She drew back and stared at him. "Are you angry?"

Adam slipped a finger down her cheek. "For what?"

"For this," she said significantly. "I, uh… I got tired of waiting for you to make the first move."

His gaze grew guarded, then he sighed and rolled into a sitting position. He offered his hand, ever the gentleman, and helped her up, as well.

A finger of uneasiness nudged her belly as the silence lengthened between them.

He looked over and smiled at her. "Did I seem angry to you?"

Er…not at the time, but she was having trouble getting a read on his mood right now. His fingers were still threaded through hers and he traced a little circle on her palm. The sensation was just as potent as the kiss they'd just shared, because he was touching her. She'd never tire of that, Winnie thought. Of feeling his skin against hers in any capacity.

"No," she finally said. "You were gratifyingly enthusiastic. But…"

He didn't look at her. "You know I'm leaving again, Winnie."

Ah… She swallowed. "Yes, I think I'm privy to that information."

He gestured at their joined hands. "I'm not altogether sure this is a good idea, under the circumstances."

Though she knew this was part of the reason he'd been holding back, a little prick of pain nevertheless pierced her heart. "Because you're leaving?"

He grimaced. "Yeah," he admitted, though she got the distinct impression there was more to it than that. The accident? Winnie wondered again. Had the funk that had put him in bed for nearly two weeks poisoned his self-worth? Winnie wondered.

She couldn't begin to imagine the trauma he'd suffered—physical and emotional. She knew he'd been in therapy while at the Center for the Intrepid because he'd made occasional remarks about the "shrink." But other than that, he hadn't confided anything to her and she hadn't asked. She didn't want to pry. To peel the scab off a healing wound.

"My hearing has been moved up to Friday," he said, sending a bolt of shock through her.

"Friday?" she asked faintly, momentarily derailed from her original line of thinking. So soon? Really? But…she wasn't ready. She didn't want him to leave. Ever, of course. But especially not right now when they were so close to having…something. She didn't have a name for it. It defied description.

He picked up a stick and dug at the ground. "I've really got to focus on getting into shape the rest of the week, you know," he said, his voice deceptively even.

In other words, he didn't have time for her. For them. And since he was leaving, it was a moot point anyway. She knew all of this was logical, that if her mind had made the leap then his keen one had seen this coming long before she had. No doubt that's why he'd been trying to avoid this suddenly awkward scenario. Still, that didn't make her feel any less miserable. It didn't make her want him any less.

But evidently…she wanted this more than he did. Because she would have been content to have had this week, to have had whatever time with him she could. To her, it wasn't pointless. It would have been a dream come true.

Winnie's cheeks burned and, though she didn't regret kissing him, she was nevertheless embarrassed that she'd so fully shown her hand. A sad smile shaped her lips. Then again, Adam had always known how she felt so the fact that she'd laid all of her cards on the table really shouldn't matter.

It shouldn't…but it did.

Winnie stood, dusted off her clothes and mentally gathered the shredded remains of her pride. "You're in great shape, Adam," she said, forcing a cheerful note to her voice that didn't ring true even to her own ears. "But I understand what you mean about needing to train." She managed a mangled smile. "No distractions, right? Gotcha." She turned and started to walk away.

She heard him stand, as well. "Winnie, wait. That's not what I—"

All of a sudden, it was just too much to take. She whirled on him. "Look, Adam, I'm sorry, okay? I don't have your strength. I don't care that you're leaving. I didn't ask you for forever. I just wanted—" She stopped, felt tears burn the backs of her lids and an ironic laugh broke from her throat. "—you," she admitted, opting for the unvarnished truth.

His expression softened. "Winnie, I—"

She sucked in another breath. "But I can see that you want something else. So I'm done throwing myself at you. You know how I feel. You know what I want. You know where I am."

Weary, but oddly relieved that she'd finally confessed her feelings, she turned again and walked away. "The ball's in your court. Do with it what you will."

Because she was done playing.

# 7

THE BALL'S IN YOUR COURT...

And that's exactly where it had sat for the past twenty-four hours.

Adam had never been more certain or more confused of anything in his life. Every word she'd said had haunted him to the point of insanity, particularly her broken but emphatic 'I want you' comment.

Was she trying to kill him? Did she have any idea how much he wanted her? How much letting her walk away cost him?

He'd had to lock down every muscle in his body to keep from going after her, God help him, to keep from showing her exactly how much strength he didn't have. Adam had been in situations behind enemy lines which hadn't required so much restraint, so much willpower.

But at what point did willpower actually become stupidity?

Adam was fighting a losing battle here—he knew

that. So why was he still resisting so damned hard? Why couldn't he give in and allow them to have what they both wanted? He only had a few days left before his meeting with Colonel Marks. If things went the way he was relatively certain they would go, he would probably be leaving early Saturday morning. No doubt there was still lots of red tape to cut through before he actually shipped out to Iraq, but all of that would be done on base. And with expediency, he imagined.

Camped out in his usual spot on the porch swing—the place he'd spent most of his time since he'd gotten home—Adam stared out over the bay and watched boats and wave-runners kick up surf. Gulls squawked and dove in and out of the water. His brother's boat, Second Helping, bobbed lazily against the dock and the sight inspired a smile and, if he were honest, a bit of loneliness and envy. He missed Levi and he missed Natalie, his best friend who his brother had married. An unlikely pairing, both of them committed to their careers, and yet they had made it work.

You and Winnie could make it work, too, a little voice whispered. You could have what they have, as well.

Adam shook his head and beat back the idea. He didn't want that…did he? Was he still so sure? Adam pondered the thought and that bronze-haired blue-eyed child he'd envisioned earlier made an encore appearance in his mind. Longing shafted through him, acute and sharp. Up until the past few days, he would have sworn that he'd never regret not having a home and family, that his career was all he'd ever really need.

But now…he didn't know.

All he knew was that he wanted Winnie, that he'd wither away and die if he couldn't kiss her again. Desire slithered through his loins and remembered heat pooled in his groin when he thought about how it had felt to have her beneath him.

Right. Perfect. Grounded. Home.

Like Levi and Natalie, a relationship between him and Winnie would have to be less than conventional. He was committed to his career and she had built a home and business in Bethel Bay that she adored. While she was not as tied to the community with responsibilities as Natalie had been, Winnie was nevertheless anchored here, as well.

She was his anchor, too.

Natalie might have kept him sane in the beginning, but nobody made him feel quite so grounded, so secure as Winnie. Simply being in the same room with her made him feel…whole. Complete. And that, admittedly, was a welcome sensation, considering that he wasn't technically whole anymore.

Strange how he didn't even think about that when

he was kissing her. He would have imagined that he would have felt a little self-conscious and clumsy, yet he hadn't given his prosthesis a second thought.

Probably because he'd been too busy thinking about how fabulous she felt in his arms.

Lean and womanly, warm and sleek. His dick stirred, remembering. His palms literally itched to feel her skin, the silken softness of her jaw. She was perfectly proportioned, as though she'd been handcrafted by a higher power expressly for him. They fit together like corresponding puzzle pieces, snug and seamless.

And God how he wanted her.

Frankly, up until this point he was proud of how well he'd managed to keep himself in check. He'd dreamt about her—both during sleep and awake—and when the waking dreams became unbearable, he'd launch into some sort of physical activity, pushing himself until he was too tired to think anymore. And in the beginning, he'd avoided her—which made him miserable and her unhappy.

Clearly that way didn't work, either.

But did it really matter? He was still going to hurt her. Regardless of what she said, Winnie wanted—and deserved—her happily-ever-after. And though he wasn't altogether certain he didn't want that himself, he knew it was still impossible. He was leaving. He'd sacrificed too much of himself for this career.

He'd earned it, dammit. He needed it.

His cell phone vibrated at his waist, thankfully distracting him. Adam checked the display and smiled. Perfect timing, he thought.

Levi.

"I'm tired of getting all of my information secondhand," his brother complained. "Why didn't you call and tell me that your appointment had been moved up?"

Adam chuckled. "Nice to hear from you, too, bro. As usual, the sound of your voice brings a tear to my eye." He sniffed dramatically.

Levi's reluctant laugh sounded over the line. "Asshole."

"I'm assuming you've talked to the General?"

"No, I talked to Mom," Levi said.

Adam blinked, a bit taken aback. Though he was certain his mother knew that there had been a change in plans, she hadn't said a word to him. She was either in denial or had finally come to accept his choice. And evidently Levi knew which option she'd taken.

Adam cleared his throat, stood up, pushed out the screen door and walked down the sloping lawn toward the bay. "Yeah? What she have to say? She's been strangely silent about it."

Levi winced. "Her feelings haven't changed, but she knows that you've made up your mind. She doesn't want to waste what little bit of time she has left with you by arguing about it."

Good, Adam thought, relieved. He didn't want to argue with her, either. It was pointless and he always walked away feeling like he'd let her down. He didn't want to disappoint her, but he couldn't be the son she wanted him to be.

"Speaking of wasting time, how are things with Winnie?"

The subject change brought him up short and made the hair on the back of his neck stand up. "What?"

"Don't play dumb," Levi said, laughing softly. "My wife is privy to all your secrets. She talked to Winnie for an hour and a half last night." He chuckled darkly. "That phone bill will be coming to you."

Winnie had talked to Natalie? About him? About everything that had happened between them? He wasn't surprised. Nat was Winnie's best friend, as well. Truthfully, had he not been so certain that he was doing the right thing, he would have called her, as well.

But he was.

It was a dead-end relationship. And no detour—as satisfying as it might be—was going to change that.

Adam swallowed. "There's nothing to tell," he said, though the lie burned his tongue.

"Bullshit," his brother replied. "From the sounds

of things you finally came to your senses and then blew it again. Don't, Adam," Levi said. His voice rang with an unusual intensity. "Winnie's crazy about you. She always has been. You're good together."

Adam didn't want to have this conversation, particularly with Levi, who was disgustingly happy at the moment. He watched a sailboat slide across the bay. "Look, I appreciate the advice, but—"

"Let me talk to him," he heard Natalie say. Muffled thumps sounded in Adam's ear as the phone was wrenched away from Levi. "Adam?"

Adam sighed and dropped his head. Oh, hell. "Hi, Nat. You keeping that big oaf of a brother of mine in line?"

"It's not easy, but yes." She drew in a deep breath, evidently preparing to let him have it. "Listen, Adam. I'm not going to pretend to know what's going on in your head. It's too complicated and I don't have time. But if you leave Winnie the way things are— with the ball in your court—so help me God I will track you down to the ends of the earth and I will hurt you. Seriously."

Though he knew she meant every word and he probably ought to feel a little worried, Adam laughed. "Nat, I—"

"Don't you Nat me, you giant ass. I am seriously annoyed with you, Adam. I mean it." She made a frustrated growl. "She's laid it all on the line for you! Do you have any idea the amount of courage that takes? Do you?" she demanded. "It's time you live up to that charm I gave you and stop being a friggin' coward."

That was the second time in the past week that someone had accused him of being a coward. Was it true? Adam knew the answer, but refused to examine the truth behind it. It was too hard. Too painful. Doubt wasn't part of his makeup. He couldn't deal with it. Not right now.

Unthinkingly, Adam reached up and fingered the charm Natalie had carved for him. The Chinese symbol for courage.

Funny, at the time she'd given it to him, he'd thought he'd need the reminder to help him get through losing part of his leg.

But there was something more, something deeper. Something he didn't want to see.

And Nat was right. Winnie had bared her soul, hadn't she? She'd made her feelings and her desires perfectly clear.

Courage, indeed, he thought, humbled.

Adam swallowed, ashamed of himself for not telling her how much he wanted her yesterday, disgusted and revolted that he'd let her walk away.

He was an utter fool. A stubborn, miserable fool.

He couldn't promise her anything—wouldn't because he didn't have anything to offer—but he would make sure that she knew she hadn't offered herself for nothing. That she hadn't been brave in vain.

He had three days left of freedom…and they were hers.

To hell with the ball, the court and the game, Adam thought as he determinedly walked back toward the house.

He just wanted her.

WINNIE EYED THE last white cupcake with chocolate frosting she'd hidden behind an éclair—she'd been saving it for Adam—and, felt her eyes inexplicably fill with tears.

How pathetic was she? Crying over a damned cupcake. Because it was his favorite. Because she'd hoped against hope that he'd want her too and come by today.

But he hadn't.

It had been a little over a day since she'd thrown the ball back into his court, and evidently he was just going to keep it and go home.

That had been a risk, she knew. But she'd be lying if she didn't admit that she'd secretly hoped that he'd want her as much as she wanted him.

That was the part that was so unbearable. That made her literally ache from the inside out. Until recently, this so-called relationship between them had always been a bit lopsided—she'd loved him and he'd considered her a pal.

But given his inability to stay away from her, as well as the veiled comments, the innuendo—the flirting—not to mention his scorching response to their kiss yesterday, she'd hoped that things were finally beginning to even up just a bit.

Clearly, that wasn't the case.

She'd all but asked him to make love to her—and he hadn't so much as strolled by her shop.

Unfortunately, until he left on Friday, she knew she'd keep hoping he would change his mind. Once he was gone and all semblance of that hope gone with him, then she would allow herself to grieve.

Jana Mulrooney poked her head into the bakery. "You still open, Winnie?"

With effort, Winnie pasted a professional smile on her face and nodded. "You just caught me. What can I get for you?"

"Petit fours," Jana said, eying the case with the maniacal sort of hunger only seen in women who were expecting.

Pregnancy hormones, Winnie thought. Once again the vision of her would-be child broadsided her—bronze curls and blue-green eyes, sooty lashes and a toothless, slobbery grin.

She let go a shaky breath and quickly filled a box. "Here you go," she said. "How are you, by the way?"

"Morning sickness sucks," Jana said. She grimaced. "Me and orange juice are no longer friends."

Winnie smiled. "Ah. And Eddie?" she asked gently.

Jana looked away and her eyes dulled a bit. "Well, he's ecstatic over the baby, of course. And he's fired his secretary."

Winnie waited. "I'm sensing a but…"

She shrugged helplessly. "I can't get past it, Winnie. Not yet. I resent that he cheated on me and I'm furious that he's ruined what should have been one of the happiest times in our marriage with this affair. He's the one who should be here, buying my petit fours for me. He should be helping me plan a nursery. I will never forget what happened. I just can't block out the memory of the day I went to tell him our happy news and caught him screwing his secretary on our old couch in his office." She shook her head. "It's just not going to happen."

No, that would definitely be hard to forget. There was no way in hell Winnie could get past something like that. But the true question, of course, was not could she forget, but could she forgive?

After a moment, Winnie decided to ask. "Do you think you will ever be able to forgive him?"

Jana shook her head and indecision was written

all over her pretty face. "I don't know. I would like to think that I could. But I'm just not sure at this point. It's still too fresh, you know?"

Winnie nodded. She certainly understood that. "So where is Eddie?"

"He's moved into the apartment over his parents' garage." She laughed. "And he's lucky they let him do that. His folks are furious at him. His mother has been reciting our wedding vows to him, repeatedly. 'What part of and keep thee only unto her did you not understand, son?'" She shook her head. "If I wasn't so angry, I would feel sorry for him."

"And the cake?" Winnie asked.

Another ghost of a smile appeared on her lips. "Ah. You'll be happy to know that I didn't give it to him at their anniversary party. I waited and gave it to him at the office the next day. In the face. In front of his cheating whore of a secretary, who also got a little bite of it, as well."

Winnie chuckled, impressed. "Excellent. I like that delivery better, too."

Jana leaned against the counter. "What about you, Winnie? Anything interesting happening with you?"

Winnie started to shake her head, but a movement outside the front of the store caught her attention. Bronze hair, broad shoulders.

Adam.

Her heart raced and her mouth went inexplicably dry.

He opened the door and sidled in. "Good. You're still here. I was afraid I'd miss you." He nodded a greeting at Jana.

"Hey, Adam," Jana said, her gaze darting significantly back and forth between the two of them. "So…thanks for the petit fours, Winnie." She gasped. "Oh, I have to pay for them."

"You can catch up next time," Winnie said. "I've already closed the register anyway."

"You're sure?"

"Sure," Winnie confirmed.

"Okay, thanks." She looked at Adam, then at Winnie and quirked a brow. "I'll see you later."

Winnie followed Jana to the door, then turned and looked at Adam. He wore khaki shorts, an off-white T-shirt and the most purposeful, determined expression she'd ever seen.

It made her heart sing.

Winnie swallowed. "If you're going to be here a few minutes, then I'm going to lock the door. I technically closed five minutes ago."

"I'm going to be here for a few minutes," Adam said. He shoved his hands into his pockets and strolled to the display case. A comical frown crossed his face when he spied the empty spot where his cupcakes were usually stored.

Despite the tension in the room, Winnie felt her lips twitch with affection. She went back behind the counter and retrieved his snack. "I always save you one," she admitted. "Just in case you come by."

He smiled and gave his head a small shake. "You're too good to me, Winnie."

She nodded primly, anticipation making her blood sing. "I know."

He chuckled softly. "So modest. It's one of your best character traits."

She smiled. "Well, since you're not particularly familiar with modesty yourself, I'm actually quite proud that you knew how to recognize it."

He licked a bit of icing from his thumb and feigned being hurt. "Ouch."

"Ha," Winnie told him. "Ouch my ass. It would take a helluva lot more than that to wound your considerable pride, you great fraud."

They'd settled right back into their familiar pattern. It was so easy to be with Adam. She felt oddly safe in his presence. Stripped bare and laid raw, but curiously protected all the same.

His gaze tangled with hers and a strange undercurrent passed between them, one she didn't quite know how to name. An expectant silence settled in the gap and Winnie found herself unaccountably nervous.

She swallowed tightly and felt her smile slip. "Was there something you wanted, Adam?"

He took a short breath through his teeth. "There was."

She waited. "Well?"

He looked away, blew out a breath and lifted his shoulders in a fatalistic shrug. When he turned back to her, his eyes were clear and thrillingly focused. He took a step forward, purposely moving into her personal space, showing her his intentions. Another electrifying jolt of happiness whipped through her.

"You," he said simply. "I want you, Winnie. I, uh… I don't have the strength to stay away from you anymore."

Joy in its purest form rushed through her. A shaky breath left her lungs. "You don't have to, Adam. I'm yours for the taking. I always have been."

An instant later, his hands were cupping her face, pushing her hair away as he slanted his lips over hers. "Good," he murmured against her mouth. She tasted his surrender—her victory—on his lips. "Because I'm about to take you."

# 8

DETERMINED THOUGH HE was—not to mention literally aching for her—Adam McPherson was nervous about being with a woman for the first time in his life.

Was it Winnie? he wondered. Or was it because he hadn't been with anyone since the accident?

Probably a combination of both, he decided, feeling her lithe body mold instantly to his. An unfamiliar emotion rushed through him, leaving a bittersweet sensation in its wake and the burn of desire running through his blood quickly seared away most of his uneasiness.

Most of the time his prosthesis felt like an extension of himself—strangely familiar now—but there was always the risk that he could move the wrong way and his foot not react accordingly.

Dammit, he should have thought about that before he came here. They needed to be careful. He'd feel terrible if he hurt her.

Furthermore, he really should have made more of

an effort to make this more special for her—take her to the beach or to their favorite secluded spot in Magnolia Park. Or hell, even McKinney Point. When he'd left his place, he'd had wonderful intentions of doing just that. But the instant he'd looked at her all of those noble objectives had simply evaporated, scorched away by the need he could no longer deny.

He wanted. He ached. He burned. And the desire to put himself between her thighs was quite honestly beyond anything in his experience—the drive, the sheer force of their chemistry demanded instant gratification. He would make it up to her, Adam thought. He would—

Winnie's hot breath sighed into his mouth and her pert breasts pressed against his chest. Her fingers traced the planes of his face, almost lovingly, then pushed into his hair and kneaded his scalp. She fed at his mouth, tangling her tongue around his, suckling, sampling, molding and with every brush of her lush lips across his, Adam felt more and more like a man and less and less like an amputee.

He inwardly marveled at the change, savored the cleansing swell of emotion washing over him.

Desire, fierce and unprecedented, chugged hotly through his veins and his dick hardened to the point just shy of pain. Tension coiled in every muscle and

▶ If offer card is missing write to: Harlequin Reader Service, P.O. Box 1867, Buffalo, NY 14240-1867 or visit: www.ReaderService.com ▶

NO POSTAGE
NECESSARY
IF MAILED
IN THE
UNITED STATES

**BUSINESS REPLY MAIL**
FIRST-CLASS MAIL    PERMIT NO. 717    BUFFALO, NY

POSTAGE WILL BE PAID BY ADDRESSEE

**HARLEQUIN READER SERVICE**

PO BOX 1867

BUFFALO NY 14240-9952

# Send For
# 2 FREE BOOKS
## Today!

## I accept your offer!

Please send me two free *Harlequin® Blaze™* novels and two mystery gifts (gifts worth about $10). I understand that these books are completely free—even the shipping and handling will be paid—and I am under no obligation to purchase anything, ever, as explained on the back of this card.

**351 HDL EYL3**          **151 HDL EYRR**

*Please Print*

FIRST NAME

LAST NAME

ADDRESS

APT.#          CITY

STATE/PROV.          ZIP/POSTAL CODE

Visit us online at
www.ReaderService.com

Offer limited to one per household and not valid to current subscribers of *Harlequin® Blaze™* books.

**Your Privacy** — Harlequin Books is committed to protecting your privacy. Our Privacy Policy is available online at www.eHarlequin.com or upon request from the Harlequin Reader Service. From time to time we make our list of customers available to reputable third parties who may have a product or service of interest to you. If you would prefer for us not to share your name and address, please check here ☐.

◄ Detach card and mail today. No stamp needed. ►

H-B-07/09

the only relief seemed to come from feeling her against him—her sleek little body and delicious rump.

He absolutely loved her ass, Adam thought, as he shaped it with both of his hands, giving her a gentle squeeze.

"Adam," she said breathlessly, tugging at his shirt. Her warm fingers brushed his belly, making him inhale sharply.

"Yes?" he asked distractedly.

She licked a path up the side of his neck, then breathed gently into his ear. "Ideally this would have happened in a bed—"

He laughed against her mouth. "Haven't you been listening? Sex and beds aren't mutually exclusive."

She chuckled, acknowledging the reminder, then licked another wicked path up the side of his neck. "Right, so the floor should appeal to your tastes."

He didn't give a damn where it took place—hell, he'd take her against the pastry case if she suggested it—so long as he got to be inside her, could bury himself in her heat right now. He was suddenly desperate, mindless with the need to feel her little body around him, her hands on his naked skin. He wanted to lick her from one end to the other, dust powdered sugar over her breasts and remove it with his tongue.

He was thankful that the back of the pastry case wasn't clear when Winnie tugged him down behind the counter, stripped his shirt over his head, then pushed him back and followed him down. Ah… Her hands slid over his chest, mapping every muscle and ridge while she kissed him—his mouth, his neck, his chest. She laved a nipple and he bucked beneath her, his breath hissing out between his clenched teeth.

But that gave him an idea…

Adam found the hem of her shirt and worked the navy blue cotton fabric up and over her shoulders and head, then tossed it aside. Her bare breasts, her pouting nipples were suddenly before him.

"No bra?" he asked, pleased. "Nice."

He tested the weight of them in his hands, then touched the tip of his tongue to the crest of one nipple, before he pulled the whole bud into his mouth.

Winnie gasped and her eyes fluttered shut. "It's b-built in," she said.

He thumbed the other nipple then sampled it as well. "What?"

"The b-bra. It's b-built into the sh-shirt."

If she still had the presence of mind to explain her undergarments, then he clearly wasn't doing this right, Adam thought. He smiled against her then suckled harder.

A startled little choking noise came from her open mouth and she flexed her hips over his, aligning the softest part of her with the hardest part of him. His dick strained against his shorts, looking for the relief that was right there, but still inaccessible.

Time to rectify that, Adam thought.

He drew her down, then slid his hands down her back, beneath her shorts and over her bare ass. His fingers encountered tiny strings and the idea made him smile.

"Thong?"

"No panty lines," she said, kissing his cheek, the edge of his mouth. A shiver seemed to run through her as he swiftly removed the tiny undies and shorts. And finally, he had what he so desperately wanted.

Winnie…naked.

Gloriously, utterly naked.

His eyes feasted on her and the sight made his chest tighten with some unnamed emotion, made his hands unaccountably shake. Bikini lines left the smallest bit of pale flesh and for reasons he couldn't begin to explain, he found this strangely sexy. He was suddenly hit with the urge to lick all those lines, to trace them with his tongue.

But Winnie had other ideas. Without warning, she reached down to unbutton his shorts and the feel of her small hand that close to his dick made it stand at attention. Though he wouldn't have thought it possible, he hardened even more. He snagged a condom from his pocket before she could remove the shorts, thankful that he'd had the presence of mind to get a package from the drugstore before coming over.

Winnie scooted down, then carefully started removing his shorts. Adam toed his shoe off, then helpfully lifted his ass so that she could finish the job. He knew a moment of uneasiness when she started to pull them down his legs. His clothes had a tendency to hang on his foot. Suddenly uncomfortable, he leaned forward to help, but she ignored him and smoothly handled the task without batting a lash.

An instant later, her hand was on him, working the slippery skin against her palm. A mere fraction of a second after that, he was in her mouth.

Adam sucked in a ragged breath and he set his teeth so hard he thought he heard a crack. He curled his hands into fists at his sides as the pleasure bolted through him.

Her mouth. On him.

Sweet hell, he didn't think he'd ever felt anything quite so wonderful. Winnie flashed her eyes—those beautiful dark blue orbs he'd seen in his dreams for the past year—at him, and the satisfaction he saw in her gaze made him want to preen with male confidence.

She lowered her lashes and took the whole of him into her mouth once more, savoring his taste on her tongue. She wore the same expression as when she ate something sweet—blissful and satisfied—and the knowledge that she was thoroughly enjoying herself, that she wanted to taste him, made him want to beat his chest and roar with primal satisfaction.

Winnie licked the length of him again, then picked up the forgotten condom, tore into the packet and swiftly rolled the protection into place.

Then she slowly—with agonizing precision—lowered herself onto him.

Adam's breath hissed out of his lungs as her moist, tight heat closed around him. Her lids drooped with the weight of pleasure and she sank her teeth into her ripe bottom lip, as though the feeling of having him inside her was almost more than she could bear.

He knew that feeling well, could claim it in every cell of his body. A curious sensation swelled in his chest, momentarily preventing him from breathing and, though he knew it wasn't entirely plausible, he'd had the strangest inkling that everything in his life was tied to this moment—his past, his future, his very existence. Everything that made him, him, was bound to her.

She was his anchor.

Winnie bent forward and kissed him again, the merest brush of her lips over his and something inside him simply…let go. Her eyes went all soft and melting as she lifted her hips and settled onto him once more.

Adam moved with her. Shaped his hands over the

sweet swell of her hips and felt her feminine muscles tighten around him in response. He loved that greedy squeeze, loved the way it made him feel.

She upped the tempo and her breath came in short little puffs. She leaned back and shoved her hands through her messy black curls, undulated her hips in the most mind-numbing fashion, like a belly dancer. Slow and sure, then swift and sexy. All the while he pushed repeatedly into her, could feel the orgasm gathering in his loins.

Oh, no, Adam thought. No way in hell was he coming before she did. It didn't matter how long it had been, Winnie deserved better than that.

And he fully intended to give it to her.

Right now.

IF WINNIE HAD ever felt anything more wonderful than their joined bodies, she couldn't recall it. Adam, her badass soldier, her love, her very heart was staring at her as though she were the most beautiful creature ever placed on this earth. And having the possessive clamp of his hands on her thighs, his mouth feeding at her breasts, was indescribably perfect.

She'd wanted this for so long…waited for so long.

He pushed up harder, increasing the tempo and she could tell that he was close. Every muscle in his gloriously proportioned body was tensed and his lips were drawn in a feral sort of smile. Dew slickened his chest, highlighting every bump, ridge and muscle.

He was, in a word, beautiful.

Achingly so.

Her chest gave a squeeze and emotion clogged her throat.

"Are you ready?" he asked, breathing hard.

Winnie tightened around him once more, then lifted her hips. "Ready for what?"

"This."

And with that enigmatic promise, he slipped his hand into her curls and found the sensitive nub hidden there.

Winnie gasped as shock and pleasure lanced through her. He rubbed against her while pushing up and the combination of the two made her entire body sizzle with sensation. She felt the beginning flash of an orgasm tingle in her womb and, like a hound catching a glimpse of a rabbit, her focus instantly narrowed. She rode him harder, panting, desperate and utterly driven by the need bearing down on her.

He bent forward and suckled her once more, rubbed her once, twice, a third time...

And then bliss.

For both of them.

The orgasm burst upon her like a rogue wave, taking her under, then lifting her back up. She tightened around him and her mouth opened in a long silent scream. Her back went straight as the convulsions pulsed through her, on and on, until finally only tremors remained and she collapsed, spent, against his chest.

Adam drew delicious circles on her back. "Wow," he said, shifting so that he could tuck her against his side. She winced as her back hit the cool tile.

"What?" he asked, instantly concerned. "Did I hurt you?"

"No," she said, cuddling closer to him. "The floor's cold."

Seemingly relieved, the frown vanished. He quickly snagged a paper towel from the open cabinet near his head, and disposed of the condom.

"Tell me about it," he told her, humor back in his voice.

She laughed. "I didn't hear you complaining before," she said, feeling more safe and secure than she ever had in her life. Why did he affect her like this? Why did she only ever feel completely protected in his arms?

His chuckle rumbled under her cheek. "Who said I was complaining. I'd put my back against a block of ice if it meant we would do that again."

She grinned. "You know there's a freezer in the back, right?"

He slung an arm over his forehead. "Bring it on. I'm ready."

Winnie leaned over him, opened the pastry case and filched a petit four. "Want one?" she asked.

"To start," he said, popping the entire thing in his mouth.

"Tsk. Tsk. You're going to choke."

"Not if you get me something to drink, too," he hinted.

Winnie licked the tiny rose off the top of another petit four, savoring the sugar on her tongue. "I don't know if you've noticed this or not, but I'm naked. If I stand up to pour you a glass of tea, I'm going to flash every person who happens to peer through my plate-glass window."

His eyes darkened appreciatively and she felt his gaze drop to her breasts. "Believe me, I've noticed."

A flush of pleasure washed over her cheeks.

"So…I was thinking we should take off for a couple of days. Would that be doable for you?"

Winnie blinked, surprised. Take off? What did he mean? "What?"

Adam slipped a finger along the top of her breast, seemingly mesmerized by its shape. "We've only got two days left," he said. "It's my fault for wasting time, but…I don't want to miss another minute with you before I—" He hesitated. "—leave."

His gaze searched hers, waiting for her answer.

Two whole days with Adam? All to herself? Winnie knew this wasn't a promise, but it was as close to one as she ever expected to get. She felt a slow smile move over her lips and the sheer happiness of this moment made her almost giddy.

"I've, uh…" She thought about what she needed to do. "I've got a couple of cakes I need to make, but Jeanette and Lizzie should be able to handle everything else." She smiled at him. "What did you have in mind?"

"Doesn't matter," Adam said, threading his fingers through hers. "I just want to breathe the same air as you."

Her heart danced. That was quite possibly the nicest, most romantic thing anybody had ever said to her, Winnie thought as a lump formed in her throat.

"We could beach it tomorrow?" he suggested. "And then take a ride up to McKinney Point?"

She grinned, pleased that he'd remembered. Winnie made a mental note to drag Adam's old parking sign out of her garage and erect it once more for this occasion. "That sounds fabulous. Can you spend the night?"

His smile was lazy and confident. "I'd planned on it."

Another dream, Winnie thought. She wondered if a person could die from happiness. Adam was at home with her, spending time with her. Going to bed with her. Being cuddled up beside her when she woke up in the morning.

At last.

And the sex… Wow. Although her experience was limited, Winnie knew what they'd just shared was extraordinary. Feeling him inside of her, his sleek skin beneath her palms, the frantic rush to climax and the sweet rain of release… It had been utterly amazing. She'd never felt so alive, so connected to another person in her life. She hadn't felt the earth move so much as her soul.

And they were going to do it again, hopefully repeatedly.

She snuggled closer to him. "Good," she finally said. "I like the idea of you spending the night."

His eyes twinkled. "Because you want to watch me sleep?"

That would be lovely, too. She blinked innocently. "You mean we're actually going to sleep?"

Adam chuckled and slapped her thigh. "I doubt it," he said. "Get dressed. We've got to get busy."

She frowned, confused. "Get busy doing what?"

"You've got two cakes to make before you can take off, right?"

"I do."

He shrugged. "So I'll help you."

She shot him a skeptical look. "You're going to help me? Bake and decorate cakes?"

"Yes. And I'll warn you now." He slipped his shorts on and reached for his shirt. "At some point tonight I'm going to paint you with powdered sugar and lick it off…very slowly."

"Oh," Winnie said, suddenly overcome by the thought. Her nipples tingled in anticipation. "How do you feel about almond icing?"

"Will it be coming off me in the same manner?"

Hell yeah. "Yes."

His grin was equally wicked. "Then it's my favorite."

# 9

"I HAVEN'T DONE THIS in years," Adam said, carefully shoring up the sand wall around his moat.

Winnie lay on her belly in the most obscene bikini he'd ever seen—probably because he knew what was underneath—and with a stone, she carefully drew a motif on their castle. They'd been at the beach since early morning and had made a full day of lying around, carousing and taking the occasional dip.

When she'd pulled out her sand-castle building tools from the back of her small SUV this morning, he'd laughed, but had to admit this was turning into the highlight of their day so far.

Then again, the day was far from over. What was to come tonight would undoubtedly knock the shine off of everything else.

"I love building sand castles," she said. "My dad is a pro at this, you know."

He remembered. Tommy Cuthbert didn't just build sand castles—he built sand-castle mansions.

Towering structures with soaring turrets. He'd pave the streets with seashells and make a drawbridge from bits of driftwood. The local kids loved simply sitting back and watching him work.

Adam frowned. "Where are your parents, by the way?" He hadn't seen them around town since he got home. He'd always sensed a bit of tension between Winnie and her mother, but she seemed to get along with her father pretty well.

Winnie smoothed out a rough spot on the sand castle and started over. A tiny frown furrowed her brow as she concentrated, and for reasons which escaped him, he found her expression ridiculously endearing.

"They bought an RV when Dad retired and have been slowly making their way out West." She grinned. "And when I say slowly, I mean slowly. They've been gone since March."

"Seriously?"

"Yep. If they find a place they like, then they settle in for a while until they get tired of it. Their ultimate destination is Alaska. They want to pan for gold." She brushed a speck of sand off her face. "Who knows how long they'll stay there."

She must miss them, Adam thought. He knew she didn't have any other family. She had no siblings and he remembered her grandparents passing away while he and Winnie had been in school.

"But they'll be back," she continued. She shot him a smile. "Everybody always comes back to Bethel Bay."

Ah. Dangerous territory, Adam thought. She was right—most people who left their small community usually returned, and he imagined he probably would, as well. Eventually. But that was decades down the road for him. His path was set on life in the military. He would go where he was needed until he wasn't needed anymore.

Adam knew this as well as his own name.

It was just his personal life that was suddenly out of focus.

While he still believed that leaving Winnie was the best thing he could do for her, Adam also knew that it was going to be one of the most difficult things he'd ever done. The ache and burn in his chest, the pall of dread that settled around him, even now was enough to make him almost choke with regret.

But…he couldn't be the man she wanted. Not ultimately.

His gaze slid over her small, athletic form and the rush of emotion he felt made him quake with its intensity. Smooth tanned skin, gleaming in the sunlight. The intriguing shadow between her breasts, the soft slope of her womanly hip. Her untidy black curls were windblown and sexy and her mouth…

Lush, plump and kissable, it was one of the most sensual things he'd ever seen.

Unable to help himself, Adam bent forward, tilted her chin up with his index finger and kissed her.

She drew back, smiling and seemingly surprised. "That was unexpected."

His broody gaze dropped to her lips again. "You have a gorgeous mouth. Sexy."

The smile faltered with the barest hint of modesty and she blushed. "Thank you." She treated him to the same sort of lingering perusal. "I happen to like that little patch of soft skin just behind your ear," she said. "It makes my insides jittery."

He frowned and fingered the part in question. "You mean here?" he asked, amazed. Aside from his mangled leg, he'd always been relatively proud of his physique. That she preferred a part of him that he hadn't truly worked on was somehow as appealing as it was annoying.

Her lips twitched and she nodded. "Yes, that's it."

He quirked a dubious brow. "Not the abs, then?" He sighed dramatically and looked away, as though wounded. "All that work for nothing."

She chuckled. "Oh, I wouldn't say that. I like those parts, as well. Actually, all of your parts are pretty damned appealing."

A thought struck. "Really? Because I seem to remember you telling me that I'd put on weight. Gone soft," he added distastefully. She'd mentioned it not long after he'd come home. It was a bit of a turning point really. She'd stopped looking at him as though she'd wanted to cry and had suddenly started treating him the same way she always had.

Then again, maybe that had just been him transferring his assumptions onto her actions. Because Winnie had never been anything but honest with him.

Winnie laughed out loud, evidently remembering. "I had to do something," she said. "You wouldn't even look at me."

Because he was trying to resist her, Adam thought. It had been futile, he realized now. He'd never stood a chance. The sudden chemistry coupled with their easy relationship—friendship, even—was more than a force to be reckoned with. He'd been powerless to resist.

And the kicker? Right now, at this moment, he didn't care. Because he was with her.

Adam winced and pushed a shell into the side of their castle. "Sorry about that," he said. "I, uh…I've been a bit of an ass."

"You have," she conceded. "But you had your reasons. You're forgiven."

She would have forgiven him regardless, he knew. She loved him. He could see it in her eyes, the soft melting look in that deep blue gaze, the barest hint of indulgence in her equally tender smile.

God, he didn't deserve her. How in the hell was he going to walk away? What kind of person was he to take advantage like this, knowing the outcome wouldn't be the one either of them wanted.

Then again, how could he not?

Winnie leaned back, stretching her spine and tilting her face toward the sun. "I love this time of day," she said. "The heat is fading, the sun is settling over the sea." She jerked her head toward the ocean. "Just look at that sky. Have you ever seen anything more beautiful?"

He had, actually. He was looking at it.

Rather than embarrass her again, he turned to look at the sky and nodded in appreciation. "It's gorgeous."

She turned toward him and smiled. "This has been fabulous," she told him, her voice wistful. "I haven't spent a whole day at the beach in years. It feels positively decadent." Her gaze slid over his chest, up his neck, along his mouth and finally settled on his eyes. "And the company hasn't been half bad, either."

"The feeling is mutual."

"Thank you," she said. "Are you about ready to head back to my place? Have a little dinner and watch that movie you mentioned?"

"I am," he told her, wondering if he could feast on

her first. Honestly, he hadn't been able to keep his hands off her today.

They'd knocked the edge off the attraction last night—he still couldn't believe they'd made it right there on the floor of her shop—and had enjoyed a repeat performance later in her back room. On a table this time. He'd never look at powdered sugar and almond icing the same way again, Adam thought, his dick twitching with remembered pleasure.

Tonight they were going to act like an ordinary couple, do ordinary things like having dinner and catching a movie. Then they would go to bed, make love, and then fall asleep. Together. Like normal couples did.

The mere thought made his chest expand with some unnamed emotion.

His gaze dropped to his leg, to the prosthesis that made them different and regret barreled through him once again.

Normal, he thought with bitter melancholy. If only.

SHE WAS READY TO go, too, Winnie thought. She hadn't been lying when she said she'd had a wonderful day, but frankly, she was in the middle of a little sexual meltdown and she needed the privacy her place would afford them. A thought struck.

"Er…have you told your parents that you won't be in tonight?"

Adam looked at her and chuckled. His hair glowed with rusty highlights in the afternoon sun and his nose and shoulders were turning a little pink. Winnie inwardly tsked. She'd warned him, the moron. But he was too tough for sunscreen.

"Actually, yes. I told them I'd be staying with a friend tonight. My mother said to tell you hi."

Winnie felt her eyes widen, then she laughed out loud. "Wow. That's…interesting."

"Does it make you uncomfortable?"

She thought about it. "No, not really. We're adults, right? I just don't want them to hate me for taking you away from them the last few days you're home."

Adam waved off her concern. "They've had me for months," he said. "Honestly, I think they're pleased." He pressed another shell into the castle, this time above the door. "They're probably getting sick of me."

She sincerely doubted that, but she wasn't surprised that Adam's parents were happy that he was making emotional progress. Even if it was only temporary— and she knew it was—Adam had at least realized that he was still man enough to make love to a woman.

And mercy could he ever make a girl feel special…

Her nipples tingled and her sex flooded with heat

at the mere thought. Winnie had always been a fan of powdered sugar, but after Adam had painted her nipples with it last night, then carefully licked it off, she could see herself becoming a little obsessive.

A shudder moved through her.

Having noticed, he frowned. "You're not cold, are you?"

She shook her head. "No, just caught a little shiver." Adam had always had that effect on her.

He looked at her for a minute longer, gauging the truth of her statement, she imagined, then looked back out toward the ocean. Kids slid on thin wakeboards in the immediate surf and seagulls darted in and around a small pool of water that had washed into a shallow spot on the beach. Music wafted in on the salty breeze and the briny scent of the ocean filled her senses. Ah…she loved the beach.

"What are you thinking?" Adam asked.

She looked at him. "What?"

"What are you thinking? I know it's the nosiest and most intrusive question in the entire history of the world, but I still want to know," he said. "I want to know what that little smile you're wearing means."

Her smile widened. "It is an intrusive question. And it's usually a woman that asks it, you know."

He dipped his chin and glared at her. "You're not implying that I am a woman, are you?"

"I have biblical knowledge that you're not," Winnie said, laughing. "I am merely pointing out that you're nosy." She waited. "Like some women."

"You're really enjoying yourself, aren't you?"

She chewed the inside of her cheek, trying not to smile. "Yep."

His deep laugh sounded, and she felt that laugh vibrate against her heart. "Well, at least you're honest about it."

"It's one of my finer qualities," Winnie told him, feigning modesty.

He snorted. "Smart ass."

"Sarcasm," she said, releasing a pent-up breath. "Just another little service I offer."

Another laugh, just as potent as the last. Sheesh, she was so pathetically in love with this man. He sighed heavily and looked at their handiwork. "What do you think?" he asked, gesturing toward the moat. "Think this baby will hold water?"

She rolled her eyes. "You built it, didn't you?"

He gave his head a small shake and smiled. "You give me entirely too much credit."

"Wrong," she said. "You don't give yourself enough."

And it was true. He genuinely didn't have any idea how extraordinary he truly was. Of course, if he did, then he probably wouldn't be quite so perfect, now would he? She much preferred him humble than arrogant. But surely there had to be a compromise there in the middle.

Adam got up, filled a bucket with water, then settled back down across from her once again. "Okay," he said. "Here we go." He carefully poured the water into the moat, making sure not to flood one area and erode the sand.

It held.

She smiled, triumphant. "I told you it would hold."

He inspected the castle. "It's quite nice. We work well together."

The compliment pleased her. "Your building skills and my attention to detail do seem to compliment one another, don't they?"

He expelled a heavy breath. "So that's that, right? We're finished?"

"Not quite," Winnie said. She picked up the small stick she'd been drawing with and drew a large window in the top of the tallest turret, then added a damsel in distress.

"What are you doing?" Adam asked.

"No castle is complete without a princess in need of rescue," she told him.

Using the same stick, she drew a horse upon the lane leading to the drawbridge and a prince atop the one-dimensional steed. She finished with a flourish.

"Ah," she sighed, smiling. "Now it's done."

Adam wore a pensive, slightly brooding expression. He looked from the princess to the prince and a line emerged between his brows. She couldn't begin to guess what he was thinking and wished at that moment that she was a mind reader. Something significant was going on in that complex brain of his and she desperately wanted to know what it was.

He reached over and took the stick away from her. "Er...in this case—for our castle—I think this whole prince saving the princess is wrong," he said, his voice slightly hoarse.

"What? Wrong?" she asked, confused.

He smoothed the hair off the princess in the turret with his finger and then, using her stick, replaced it with short, wavy curls reminiscent of his own.

Winnie's throat tightened.

Next, Adam moved onto the man on horseback. He studied Winnie's hair for a moment, then applied the tool to the prince, changing the locks on that figure, as well. He added the distinct silhouette of a breast and did something to the eyes to make them appear bigger, more feminine.

He looked up at her then and the gratitude she saw in those beautiful blue-green eyes made a lump the size of a golf ball form in her throat.

"See," he said, as though it wasn't a big deal, as

though he hadn't just shared a major revelation at all. "The princess saves the prince in this story." He nodded once and gave the castle another once-over. "It's perfect now."

Winnie merely nodded, unable to speak.

Yes, she thought. Yes, it was.

# 10

It seemed incredibly odd to Adam that he'd been friends with Winnie for years, but had never set foot in her house. The small dark green craftsman was two blocks from town, a five minute walk to her bakery. And, much like her shop, it had her whimsical sense of style all over it.

"Home sweet home," she said, shooting him a nervous look as she mounted the back porch to open the door. Fanciful wind chimes—spoons and forks, crystals and glass, copper and beads—hung in one foot intervals around the perimeter of the porch and a huge painting of a mermaid lounging on the beach had been hung on the wall. A colorful rug, complete with fringe, had been painted onto the floor and a sign that read "I like my crazy" hung above the back door.

The sentiment made him chuckle. Only Winnie.

She followed his gaze and grinned. "What?" she said, her eyes playful. "I do like my crazy."

He did, too. Her crazy was sexy. "Did you paint that?"

She nodded as though it should be obvious. "You can't find that sort of quality artwork just anywhere, you know."

He laughed again and followed her inside. "Right."

The kitchen was outfitted in fifties décor. The same harlequin pattern that covered the bakery floor was here, as well. Old red and white aprons had been fashioned as curtains over the sink and cherries seemed to be either painted or printed on most of her décor. The only nod to modernization at all was her appliances and countertops. They were all sleek stainless steel.

An orange and white tabby the size of a small toddler waddled into view and meowed loudly. Its face looked like it had been walloped with a frying pan.

Winnie bent and rubbed the feline behind its ears. "Sorry, Fido." She winced. "You're on a diet."

Adam snorted. "You've named your cat Fido?"

She grinned at him, then stood and shrugged. "I liked the irony."

He had to admit he did, as well. As for the diet, the enormous feline definitely needed to be on one. He didn't think he'd ever seen a cat quite so…large.

"He's huge," Adam remarked.

"I know. He's a glutton. The vet finally said it was

time to intervene." She glanced at him, endearingly unsure. "You want to see the rest of the house?"

"I'd love to," Adam said, following along for the tour.

The living room was loaded with comfy furniture and an eclectic mix of antiques. He spied the flat screen television mounted above her fireplace—which at the moment was filled with assorted candles—and nodded with satisfaction. A bat hung from a wrought-iron arm mounted to the wall and a collection of colored glass globes in varying sizes and shapes were suspended in her wide, living room window. Books and magazines were stacked in tidy piles and a pair of funky reading glasses lay on her coffee table.

"What's with the bat?" he asked.

She lifted one shoulder. "I just liked him."

Adam merely grinned and shook his head.

"The bedrooms and bathroom are this way," she told him, leading him into a small hall.

The bathroom held an old clawfoot tub—shower attached above—and black-and-white toile covered the walls. Simple, but effective. Little glass knobs had been added, holding her towels, robe and whatnot. A soft floral smell emanated from the room, the same scent as her hair. The thought made him smile.

"Nice," Adam said, nodding toward the tub. "That looks big enough for two."

"Probably," she said, and he had the pleasure of watching her eyes darken with desire. "I've never tried it."

Oh, they'd need to rectify that, Adam thought, sidling closer to her. "That's easy enough to remedy."

She flushed. "The b-bedrooms are over here," she continued. She pointed to a room on his right. "This is the guest room, which I tend to use as more of a closet. The closets are tiny in these old houses."

He grunted, barely noting the green spread and peacock tapestry above the headboard. "That's because people didn't have as much crap."

"True," she said, gesturing toward the other door. "And this is my room."

Intensely curious about this particular space, Adam peered around the doorframe and absorbed every detail. A huge four-poster shaker-style bed stood in front of a large window. Dark purple velvet hung in curtains around it, though they'd been tied back at the moment. A velvet coverlet and cream and silver pillows were scattered over the surface.

A silver filigree jewelry box, a picture of her and Natalie and a picture of Fido sat on her mirrored dresser. A pair of running shoes were tucked in the corner against the wall and a black lacy bra hung on the closet doorknob. Art deco prints of half-naked women dressed the walls and purple tassels dangled from the lampshades. It was lush and decadent and feminine…just like Winnie.

Desire broadsided him and the bed loomed large before him. They were a mere five steps from that bed, five measly seconds away from heaven. He'd been waiting for hours to take her again, to lose himself in the welcoming tight heat of her sweet little body.

He didn't have to wait any longer.

He felt Winnie's hands come around his bare midriff and her lips pressed between his shoulder blades.

He quaked beneath that tiny kiss, felt it resonate to his very soul.

Unable to hold back, Adam turned around, scooped her up and carried her to that magnificent bed. He carefully laid her down, kissing her all the way, then aligned his body with hers.

She was still in the bikini top and bottoms, with only a matching skirt around her waist, so it took very little time and less effort to remove her clothing. His too, for that matter. He was getting better at this, Adam thought absently. He kissed her sun-warmed skin and the saltiness burst over his tongue. He savored it. Lapped it up. God, she tasted good. He laved a nipple and suckled deep. He felt her hand close around him, guiding him to her center and he'd just nudged those weeping folds when reality intruded.

"Condom," he breathed against her mouth, going utterly still.

Winnie winced and lifted her hips, seeking his weight. "I'm safe and protected," she told him, her pupils all but entirely edging out the blue. "Are you?"

"Completely," he said, searching her gaze.

She rocked against him once more. "Then what are you waiting for? Come into me." She framed his face with her hands, leaned up and kissed him.

Adam thrust forward and entered her in one smooth, sure stroke. Her tight heat fisted around him and the sensation was so unbelievably wonderful that he locked his knees and stayed still for a moment, relishing the feel of being completely enveloped—fully surrounded—by her.

Winnie's breath leaked from her lungs as he'd pushed in and she seemed to be holding what was left of it as she stared deeply into his eyes. Hers were soft and melting and full of love and desire. He hoped she could see the same emotion reflected back at her.

He had never in his entire misbegotten life felt anything as wonderful as this. Had never felt more complete, more secure or more loved. More grounded.

Ever.

She was his anchor, he thought again.

And it was a good thing that she was holding him now, because he was in serious danger of just floating away on the cloud of sheer happiness he found himself on. It ought to be a crime to feel this good, Adam thought. To have someone love you the way she loved him.

Winnie tightened around him again and lifted her hips, pulling him in deeper. A slow cat in the cream pot smile slid over her beautifully carnal lips and the breath she'd been holding finally released. She slid her hands down his shoulders, along the fluted hollow of his spine, then over his ass. She gave a gentle, territorial squeeze—the same kind he'd treated her to last night—and that was all it took to send Adam racing for release.

He drew back and pushed again, harder and faster, harder, faster and she caught his rhythm and met him thrust for thrust. She let loose tiny moans of pleasure as she bent forward and licked his throat, then sank her small teeth into his shoulder.

The little nip did strange things to him, tripped a trigger he hadn't known existed. Three delicious thrusts into her body later, the most forceful orgasm he'd ever experienced in his life exploded out of him.

Come into me, indeed, Adam thought as he quaked with the aftermath.

He'd filled that order, by God.


"YOU DIDN'T HAVE to choose a military movie," Adam chided hours later as the final credits rolled.

Winnie snuggled against his side, more content than she could ever recall. After their impromptu sex in her bedroom, they'd shared a bath in her claw-foot tub and the orgasm she'd missed in the bedroom was given back to her twofold, along with the strong warning never to bite him again unless she wanted to end things prematurely. He'd been satisfied, but embarrassed that he'd lost control and left her hanging.

Of course, now that she knew this was an effective way to set him off, Winnie fully intended to press her advantage whenever the opportunity presented itself.

She leaned over and nipped at him now, enjoying hearing his breath leave in a strangled hiss.

"Winnie," he warned.

She drew back and blinked innocently. "What?"

"You know what. You've been nibbling on me all through the movie. Do you know how disconcerting it is to be watching Gene Hackman and get a hard on?" He grinned, outraged. "Please, woman. You're killing me."

Winnie chuckled. "S-sorry," she said. "But I like it."

"I like it, too," he said, sounding surprised. "All the same, there is a time and a place for everything, and when Gene and Denzel are on the flat screen isn't it."

She laughed again and slapped his thigh. He hadn't been the least bit self-conscious about his leg today, even when they'd negotiated the bathtub, which had surprised her. All the same, she'd given him some privacy, covertly watching from the mirror. It still hurt her when she saw the angry scars on his leg, but the fact that she was so thankful that he'd adjusted so well assuaged most of the regret.

"I don't mind watching military movies," she said. She gave him a quick smile. "Besides, after Natalie made you sit through Steel Magnolias, I didn't have the heart to petition for a chick flick." She slid him a sly glance. "Is it true you cried?"

He glared at her, but his smile lessened the effect. God, how she loved that grin. It did things to her insides that ought to be a criminal offense. Made her thighs quake and her belly go all warm and melting.

"I did not cry, dammit. I'm going to kill her for that. I don't cry," he insisted. "It's ridiculous."

Her antennae twitched. "What do you mean you don't cry?"

He blinked and looked away, then fiddled with the remote control until he found the ten o'clock news. "I don't cry," he said simply. The muscles in his throat worked as he swallowed a bit of the tension that tightened his jaw. "Couldn't tell you the last time I shed a tear."

Wow, Winnie thought, torn between being impressed and unsettled. She managed a shaky laugh. "I'm a weeper," she confessed. "I cry when I see sad commercials, when I finish a hard-won race, when I stub my pinkie toe," she said, gesturing wearily. "I'm a wuss."

Her gaze inexplicably slid to his leg, back to the scars that puckered his flesh. What sort of willpower did it take not to cry when something like that happened? When you woke up from surgery and part of your leg was gone? When you realized that your career—your very way of life—was over?

He hadn't cried?

Seemingly unsettled by her silence, Adam turned to look at her and released a small breath. He swallowed. Passed a hand over his face. She hated when he looked like this, so unsure. It was so out of character it was heartbreaking.

"It's not that I'm some sort of heartless badass, Winnie," he said. "But…what I've gone through is nothing—nothing—compared to what I've seen others endure. It would be a disservice to them to weep for myself."

Ah… Noble again, her wounded warrior, but his thinking was flawed. "You could always weep for them, too."

He blinked, seemingly startled at her suggestion.

"I do," she said. "It's one of the few things that I can actually do, if that makes sense. Tears are the truest form of compassion." She looked away, picked at a lose thread on her shorts. "I hope no one ever thinks my tears are a disservice," she said. "Because they certainly aren't meant that way. They're shed in gratitude—" her voice broke "—but never pity. Pity would be a disservice."

Adam threaded his fingers through hers and was silent for a moment. She got the impression that he was considering her opinion, which made her feel slightly encouraged. She sincerely hoped she'd gotten through to him, corrected a bit of that faulty thinking.

Rather than push her point, she leaned over and pressed a kiss to the underside of his jaw. "Come on," she said. "Let's go to bed."

This was her one and only shot of waking up in Adam's arms. Initially, Winnie had thought of setting a grand seduction, of trying to round up lingerie and candles and turning on mood music. She'd wanted to make the night memorable somehow, commemorate their one and only full night together. But then something profound had occurred to her.

They didn't need it.

The beauty in this night would be found in the simplicity—in the normality—of it instead.

When she thought about the fact that Adam would walk out of her life tomorrow, it was all she could do to hold it together. To pretend for his sake that this was going to be enough. That this little slice of heaven was all she wanted when in truth she wanted the whole thing—marriage and a family, making love and making up, holidays and every days, clambakes and picnics and long runs at sunset. She wanted to build more sand castles and hold his hand, feel the warmth of his mouth against her temple.

She wanted to be loved. To be adored. By him. Until they drew their last breath.

Was that so much to ask? Winnie wondered.

Adam turned to her and smiled and the simple re-arrangement of his mouth into that grin made something in her belly flutter, her breath catch. "Bed sounds nice," he murmured. "I'm ready when you are."

The promise in his low voice made her heart pound.

And there was absolutely nothing ordinary about that.

# *11*

ADAM WATCHED WINNIE go about the routine of readying for bed and something about the mundane task, knowing that she did this every night, made him feel privy to a secret part of her only he was allowed to see. She hadn't told him that he was the only man who'd ever spent the night in her bed—who'd been invited and welcomed into her private domain—but he knew it all the same.

The mere idea made him want to beat his chest and roar, then go outside, walk around her house and piss in every corner of the yard. He shook his head wryly. That would certainly give her neighbors something to talk about.

She quickly loaded their popcorn bowls and glasses into the dishwasher, made sure Fido had water, locked the doors and finally turned off the television. She shot him a hesitant smile. "You want the bathroom first?" she asked.

Adam shook his head. "You go ahead."

She released a small breath. "I'll only be a minute."

While she was otherwise engaged, Adam took the opportunity to gather his toiletries from his bag and smiled when he encountered the condoms. I'm safe and I'm protected.

Hands down, those had to be some of the most beautiful words he'd ever heard in his life. Sliding into her, feeling her hot, feminine muscles clamping around him…

Sweet God, the sensation had shaken him to his very soul.

Unparalleled and completely perfect, it had rendered every other pleasurable memory obsolete.

Winnie chose that moment to come walking into the bedroom. Her face was scrubbed clean, her nose shiny, and she brought the scent of mint and something else—that floral scent he'd never been able to get out of his head—with her. She wore a pair of tiny white cotton panties with hot-pink polka dots and a matching tank.

His breath caught in his throat. She was sexy and fresh and good—utterly and completely good—and God help him, he was leaving her tomorrow night.

The weight of that realization bore down on him like a Mac truck and it was all he could do to force his mouth into a smile and nod at her as he made his way to the bathroom. Adam shut the door, then braced either side of his hands on the sink and stared at his wretched reflection.

He could get through this, Adam thought, drawing on the last of his reserves. It was the only way. He'd known it when he surrendered. Known that he was leaving, that he would have to walk away from her.

No, he was leaving Bethel Bay, going back to a job he loved, one that defined him. One that had been his purpose since he was old enough to have one.

Winnie… Winnie deserved so much more. She deserved a man who would be here for her…and he would despise and envy that lucky bastard, whomever he turned out to be.

He could not be hers. He could not have her, dammit.

Beyond this last little bit of time they had left, at any rate.

And he was wasting it, chasing the only conclusion around in a circle in his mind when she was waiting for him in bed.

Winnie had waited for him long enough.

Resolved, Adam quickly washed up and brushed his teeth. Thirty seconds later he was standing in the doorway to her room and the sight she made would forever be indelibly printed on his brain. Purple velvet, bare shoulders, wild black curls. She was laying on her side and had turned the covers down for him in open invitation.

Every care in the world rolled off his shoulders at that wanton look and a sigh of contentment suddenly welled from somewhere deep within. He stripped off his shirt, then sidled forward, sank onto the edge of the bed and started to remove his prosthesis. He'd done it several times in her presence now and, though it had felt a bit odd at first, Adam had to admit that, other than the vaguest sense of insecurity—which came every time he took it off—it didn't signify anymore. He leaned it against her bedside table, then carefully stripped away the sock, leaving himself bare.

Winnie pressed a kiss to his back and her arm snaked around his middle, rolling him to her.

And that was all it took to lose himself in her.

Her scent, the silken feel of her skin. Crisp sheets and sleek velvet, the rustle of both fabrics as she climbed smoothly on top of him. Her hot mouth on his neck, his cheek, sighing into his ear.

Adam groaned. "A novel change, doing this in bed," he murmured, dragging her shirt over her head and tossing it aside. He suckled her breast and had the pleasure of feeling a shudder move through her. He loved those little sounds, those little markers that he was doing something right.

"I've dreamed about doing this in this bed more

times than I can count," Winnie confided in a breathless gasp. The admission made his chest fill with masculine satisfaction.

Adam flipped her over, then kissed his way down her belly, licked a lazy swirl around her belly button, then made a determined trek toward the heart of her sex.

Winnie shuddered as he parted her dark curls. "A-Adam," she said brokenly.

He blew against her and smiled as she lifted her hips in anticipation.

"Do you know what I've dreamed about, Winnie? What's haunted my dreams for the past fifteen months?" He touched the tip of his tongue to the little nub nestled at the top of her sex and her taste washed over his palate, all musk and woman, drugging him with its potency.

"N-no," she said, fisting her hands in her sheets. "Tell m-me."

He smiled and licked her fully. "Better yet, I'll show you." Then he settled in and feasted on her, lapped and laved and suckled. "This and this and this," he said, between tastes. He pushed a finger deep inside her incredibly tight channel and hooked it around, searching for that one place—

She bucked against him and he smiled.

Found it.

Adam tented his tongue and worked it against her while massaging that tiny patch of sensitive skin hidden deep within. Winnie's breath came in hard little puffs and her thighs alternately went rigid and quaked.

"Adam— If you don't— I can't take—" Then she moaned low and a scream of pure ecstasy ripped from her throat.

Adam slowed his assault, licking her lazily.

She melted into the mattress. "That was—I've never—" Breathing hard, she pushed her hands through her hair. She laughed shakily. "Wow. That was impressive."

Adam crawled up the length of her body and smiled down at her. "Baby, you ain't seen nothing yet."

IF HE ADDED ANY more wickedness to that lethal smile of his, she'd be nothing more than a puddle of goo.

Oh, wait. She already was.

Still spent, tingling and trying to recover, Winnie bent forward and nipped at Adam's shoulder. She could feel him nudging the inside of her thigh, but was curiously consumed with the desire to taste him, as well. Hadn't she wanted to feel the silken heat of him in her mouth?

He bent and nuzzled the underside of her breast, sending another delicious shiver through her. Her eyes fluttered shut, absorbing the pleasure until she decided that there was no time like the present to do something she wanted to do.

Oh, yeah.

Tugging at her nipple with his teeth now, Winnie framed his face and drew him away. "Turnabout's fair play, right?"

He blinked, seemingly dazed. Those clear eyes were heavy-lidded and darkened with desire and the idea that she'd done this to him sent a little thrill straight into her heart.

Before he could sort it out, Winnie twisted herself around, took him in hand…then in her mouth.

Adam swore hotly and that little release of self-control made her inordinately pleased. Emboldened, she swirled her tongue around the engorged head, then licked him slowly from root to tip. She cupped his balls and heard another word—one she didn't think she'd ever heard come from his mouth before—leave his lips in a hiss of haste.

"Winnie," he said warningly.

She took him fully in her mouth, working her tongue along his shaft and relished the feel of his hot, slippery skin against her lips. Her body went all limp and languid again and an answering tingle buzzed through her weeping sex. She upped the tempo, lick-ing, laving, sucking and worked him against her palm, her mouth chasing her own hand.

Adam locked his muscles, his thighs went rigid. She felt him harden against her mouth and tasted the salty essence leaking from the tip.

"Winnie," he choked out again. "If you don't stop—"

She laughed against him. "You'll what?"

A maniacal chuckle bubbled from his chest and she could feel him twitch, could sense the orgasm building in his loins, could taste the impending release.

"You know what," he said harshly. Unable to take anymore, he leaned forward, grabbed her arms and flipped her once more onto her back. She'd barely taken a breath before he thrust into her.

"Ahhhh," he sighed, angling deep.

Winnie literally felt her eyes roll back in her head. A gasp caught and held in her throat. She wrapped her legs around his waist, then grabbed the twin globes of his ass and simply absorbed the feeling of having him inside of her.

Perfect. Flawless. Without blemish.

He bent and pressed a series of kisses along her jaw, punctuating each little caress with a determined thrust. Slow and steady, deep and sure.

God, he felt wonderful.

She squeezed his ass, and pushed up against him, trying to drag him more completely into her. She didn't want to know where he ended and she began, she didn't want to be aware of anything but the feel of his body—sleek skin, supple muscle, beautifully masculine—inside her own.

Winnie slid her hands over his back, along the narrow corridor of his spine, over his wide shoulders, then pushed her hands into his hair and brought his mouth down to hers for another kiss. His chest heaved against hers, abrading her nipples and her breasts bounced, absorbing the force of each thrust.

Harder and faster, he pushed and pushed and she could feel herself spiraling out of control again. He kindled the flame of orgasm and fanned it determinedly with each magnificent press of his body into hers.

Adam grabbed her hands, threaded his fingers through each one of hers and stretched them up above her head. Something about the movement shifted things between them—physically and emotionally— and she felt it on every level of her soul. He was laying her bare, making her vulnerable and she wanted that if it meant she could be his. She'd give everything to him, wouldn't leave a single bit of herself left over.

She was his for the taking. Always had been. Always would be.

She arched up, flexed her hips against his, taking more and more of him.

Adam groaned, a masculine purr that made her feel distinctly feminine. A rare thing for a girl who was essentially a tomboy at heart. Maybe that's what made him so special, Winnie thought, as the revelation unfurled like a morning glory to the rising sun. Maybe that's why she felt so safe and protected with him?

Because she never felt like less of a girl when she was with him. She was always just…herself. Adam had given her the freedom to do that. To just be.

She smiled up at him and tightened around him as this newfound understanding wrapped itself around her heart, settling over her like a warm blanket.

Adam's gaze tangled with hers and something about his territorial expression, the utter awe and defenselessness she saw in his gaze made the orgasm that had hovered just out of reach suddenly bear down on her. Her breath came in hard, labored little puffs and with every hammering blow he laid into her body, she got closer and closer, could feel release nearing the breaking point deep inside of her.

"Adam," she groaned. "I need—I want—"

She bucked beneath him, tightened once more, holding on to him as he plunged in and out, in and out.

Without warning, he leaned forward and nipped at her skin, biting the sensitive flesh where neck met shoulder.

She shattered.

Wave after wave of sensation pulsed through her. Her mouth opened in a scream and she was surprised to discover that it wasn't soundless, but tore from her throat with all the force of a battle cry. Her vision darkened around the edges, everything faded to gray, then black, then back to vivid color, shades she would have sworn she'd never seen before. Her body fisted around him and with every contraction of her orgasm, he continued to hammer into her, dredging every bit of pleasure he could from her.

Oh, no, Winnie thought. She wasn't going to be the only one to literally come apart.

She leaned up and bit him, as well, a gentle nip that had instant and desired effect.

A guttural cry ripped from his chest and he seated himself so firmly into her she imagined it would take the Jaws of Life to get him out. She felt him shudder above her, his magnificent frame tense and shiver. Her badass, her wounded warrior, Winnie thought, as warmth pooled deep in her womb, igniting another little sparkler of pleasure.

Adam looked down at her and the emotions she saw reflected back at her made a lump well in her throat. She bent forward and kissed him, lingering until the moment it was almost too bittersweet to take.

With a soft sigh, he rolled off her, then dragged her up against his chest.

Contentment weighted her limbs and lids and she fell asleep listening to the sound of his heart beat—the most reassuring sound in her world—beneath her ear.

# *12*

ADAM AWOKE THE NEXT morning with the feel of a soft, womanly body bellied up to his back, a sleek thigh pressed between his legs and an extremely large tabby cat curled around the top of his head.

In the time it took to mentally review and place all three, a smile was already sliding over his lips and images from the night before came rushing back to him, making him wish for a morning repeat.

Without the cat, he thought, feeling Fido's tail swish across the top of his head.

Warm skin, supple breasts, her hot tight heat…

Winnie's sweet palm lay curled against his chest and he could feel her soft, reassuring breath between his shoulder blades. Morning light spilled across her bed, bathing the room in a clear glow. Though he would love to turn over and look at her sleeping face, wondering what secrets he might discover in the relaxed visage, Adam didn't want to risk waking her up.

A glance at the bedside clock confirmed the time—eight-thirty. Despite the fact that he didn't want it to, reality soon intruded. The idea that he would be sitting in front of Colonel Marks this time tomorrow made him inwardly tense with regret.

Their time together was circling around, getting smaller and smaller, Adam thought, unwilling to name the ache that suddenly formed in his too tight throat. He swallowed tightly and bit it back.

He couldn't think about that now. He'd have to think about it later, when he was alone. He would not spoil their remaining day together by being depressed over the inevitable outcome.

He was leaving. She was staying. This was the way it had to be.

They both had to move on.

Winnie would be better off, Adam tried to tell himself. She would grieve and mourn, of course— so would he—but ultimately she would heal and find someone else. Particularly if he didn't leave her a choice. The idea of someone else taking his place in her life, his place in her bed, was more repugnant to him than he could have ever imagined. The absolute fury of the thought made him set his jaw so hard he thought his molars would crack.

Someone else…right here…with Winnie.

Her arm around someone else, her breasts against

someone else's back, her leg insinuated between someone else's thigh.

Bile rose behind his teeth and the revulsion was almost impossible to swallow.

Dammit all to hell.

Adam knew that he was lucky to be alive, and even luckier that he'd only lost part of his leg. As far as amputee cases went, the fact that he'd been able to keep his knee had made his recovery and prognosis so much better than for those who didn't. He had many things he should be thankful for.

But at the moment, he was having a hard time hanging on to that sentiment.

Because someone else would ultimately have his Winnie. And though he wasn't ready to admit it to himself—couldn't, dammit—he knew there was more to this than his irrational commitment to his career. Feelings of inadequacy as a result of the accident had been stirring in the back of his brain for months, but he'd refused to acknowledge them, telling himself that he was fine. He had to prove that he was normal. That he could be the same guy. And that same guy had never planned on this.

On Winnie.

As if he'd called her name, she stirred behind him, slid her knee further between his legs and cuddled closer. He knew the exact moment when she awoke because her breathing changed—hitched a bit—then settled back into rhythm.

He put his hand over hers and squeezed. "Morning," he said, his voice rusty.

"Hmm," she agreed sleepily.

Unable to help himself, he turned to face her. Morning light gleamed over her messy, black curls and painted her skin with an ethereal glow. Her lips were soft and pink and a wash of color stained her cheeks. If he'd ever seen anyone so beautiful in his life, he couldn't recall it.

Adam smiled at her. "You're gorgeous, you know that?"

Her dark blue eyes widened with surprise, then the color deepened. She lowered her lashes, looking away. "Thank you."

He blinked as a thought occurred to him. "I've never told you that before, have I?"

She bit her bottom lip and gave her head a small shake. "Not that I can remember, no."

And she would have remembered, he knew. Adam tsked under his breath and shook his head. "I'm sorry. I've always thought it, you know? Even before the night we shipped off last year."

And he had. While admittedly he'd never been romantically interested in her until then, he'd always been aware of how finely she was made. She had an interesting face. Wide forehead, heavily lashed blue eyes with a slight slant that neatly harmonized with her cheekbones. Smallish chin and the mouth… A mouth that was what wet dreams were made of. It was shockingly sexy.

Seemingly intrigued, Winnie peered over at him. "You did? Really?"

"I did."

"Hmm."

What sort of hmm was that? Adam wondered. He frowned. "What do you mean hmm?"

"You never said anything."

"I was a fool." He smiled. "And at the time I was a lot more interested in getting a hit off your knuckle ball than looking at your ass." He reached down and filled his hand with a cheek. "Which is also especially fine."

She chuckled wryly. "Yes, well. I'm sure there isn't anything I can tell you that I haven't told you before."

He'd certainly had the advantage there, Adam thought. While she'd never been particularly vocal or forthright with her feelings, Adam had never had to wonder about how Winnie Cuthbert felt for him.

She'd loved him for as long as he could remember.

He'd said it to her a minute ago, but it beared repeating. "I was a fool."

Winnie ran the pad of her cool finger along his jaw. "Yes, but you've always been my fool."

And he was a fool for her now. Too little too late.

Evidently sensing the change in his mood, she cuddled next to him once more. "So…what's on the agenda today?"

"You mean aside from going up to McKinney Point and having my wicked way with you so that we can fulfill one of your secret wishes?" He looked down at the floor. "I've, er…" He hated to bring this up, but it couldn't be avoided. "I need to go home for a couple of hours and pack." His mother, the saint, had been doing his laundry for the past couple of days in preparation.

Winnie went utterly still. "Pack? You mean you're not coming back tomorrow afternoon?"

Damn. He should have mentioned this sooner. "No," he admitted reluctantly. "I'm relatively certain of the outcome. I'll get new orders. There will be a bit of paperwork that will need to be taken care of on base, so to expedite matters I'll stay there until I go back to Baghdad."

"Oh."

One word and it slayed him.

"I…see." Winnie sat up and looked away from him. "Excuse me a minute," she said, her voice hoarse. "Erm… Nature calls."

Dammit, he'd made her cry, he thought as she darted naked to the bathroom. The sound of the faucet rang out like a gunshot in the quiet house. Behind him, Fido meowed loudly, twitched his tail, then dropped from the bed and went in search of Winnie.

A few minutes later, her lashes a bit wet, she donned an off-center smile and came back into the bedroom. "So when were you planning on going home today then?"

"Winnie you don't have to pretend for me, okay? I know you're upset." He felt like a first-class bastard.

Her smiled slipped. "I am," she admitted. "You know my heart as well as I do, Adam, so I don't have to explain why." She drew in a bracing breath. "But I agreed to your terms—happily," she emphasized, her voice breaking. "And I'm not wasting a single moment that I have left with you crying over the fact that you're leaving. You're here now," she said. "And for now, that's all that matters."

"Are you sure?"

A sad smile touched her lips. "You know better than to even ask me that."

He blew out a breath. "I actually thought I'd head over this morning and get everything put together."

He had another errand too, one that he was desperately determined to see to now. He wanted to get her something, a small token of his gratitude. If she hadn't barged into his bedroom two weeks ago, who knows what might have happened to him? Winnie had dragged him from the edge of the unknown and set him back on the path he was meant to tread.

She nodded once. "Okay. So you'll be back later, then?"

"Most definitely. I'm yours until…"

Another sad grin. "Until you have to go," she finished.

He nodded once more, dreading that moment more than he had anything else in his entire life.

WINNIE DROPPED ADAM off at his house and, with a sinking heart and the sound of the clock ticking loudly in her mind, reversed out of the drive and made her way back to her own little cottage.

Into her garage, specifically.

Though she'd taken Adam's parking spot sign down when he'd gone away to college, she'd been unable to throw it into the trash. Too many hours spent agonizing over the paint and thinking about the girls he'd taken up to McKinney Point had made it nearly impossible to chuck into the garbage like any normal woman would have done.

But Winnie was not normal.

She'd been neurotically in love with the same guy for more than a decade. That feeling had never shaken, waned or wavered. Not once, in spite of the fact that he'd never returned those feelings.

Or at least he hadn't…until now.

Winnie didn't know what sort of change had come over Adam, didn't know the exact moment when he'd fallen for her, too, but she knew beyond a shadow of a doubt that he had. She could read it in every look, feel it in every touch. She saw it when those wonderful eyes went soft and indulgent, felt it when he pressed an affectionate kiss to her cheek. The tender way he tugged her to him, the playful sling of his shoulders around hers. He was happy with her. Truly, genuinely happy.

And this wasn't a product of wishful thinking or false hope.

Adam loved her.

Whether he knew it or not.

Thankfully, years of observing his behavior had served her in good stead. She knew the best possible thing she could do at the moment was simply be herself. To take what he was giving her.

Despite the excuse Adam maintained—the fact that he was leaving—Winnie knew something else was at play here. Things, she suspected, he hadn't even admitted to himself. In many ways he was the same old Adam, the confident, irreverent, driven boy she'd fallen in love with long ago.

But in other ways—particularly since the accident—he was different.

There was a weariness around his eyes that never truly left, an occasional haunting expression when she wondered if he was reliving the horrific event. Adam was clinging to the life he'd had before almost too hard, as if the injury would swallow him whole if he made any concessions for it at all.

Admittedly this morning when he'd told her that he wouldn't be returning to Bethel Bay after his meeting, she'd had a little meltdown. She'd thought that they'd have some time together before he actually left for Iraq. More time to work him around to her way of thinking, to convince him that he didn't want to be without her.

No doubt Adam thought a clean break would be in both of their best interests—particularly hers—and that was more than likely the reasoning behind his decision to remain on base. She'd faltered when he'd told her because she'd counted on that additional time, had grown attached to it even, and didn't want to miss a minute with him before he boarded a flight bound for the Middle East.

His change to her plans had thrown her into an emotional tailspin, and she'd suddenly found herself on the verge of breaking into tears, which would have been unacceptable behavior on her part. It would only serve to make him feel guiltier and all the more determined to go before doing her further damage.

Noble idiot, she thought, stashing the sign and a rubber mallet in the back of her SUV. She slid behind the wheel and made her way up to McKinney Point, found Adam's old spot and replanted the sign.

Ah, Winnie thought, as the mallet swung limply from her hand. Now this is more like it. She'd suffered endless hours of agony wishing that he'd been up here with her, desperately hoping that she could be the girl in his arms, the girl who was helping him fog up the windows in his old Chevy.

Weekend after weekend, hour after hour, girl after girl.

A slither of satisfaction moved through her veins. It was her turn, by God, and she had every intention of taking it while she could. Furthermore, she was just competitive enough to want their time together up here to obliterate the memory of any other girl in his head.

And if she had to act like a bonafide tramp to make it happen, then she would.

Winnie was staking her claim.

He might be determined to leave her and never come back, but dammit, she was going to make it hard for him. Leaving her—leaving what they could be—would not be easy.

She wanted him to fight for her, to fight for them.

The fact that he could take his prosthesis off—an act that made him more vulnerable than anything else—and spend the night in her bed ought to tell him that he was safe with her. More specifically, that they were safe.

Last night when he'd settled onto the bed and started to remove his leg, she'd watched the anxiety race across his face—the barest hint of fear—and tried to imagine herself in his place. Tried to imagine the fear of needing to act in an instant, get up from bed…and realize that she couldn't. The thought absolutely terrified her. Granted he could be into the leg in less than ten seconds, but that didn't lessen the knowledge that he was completely vulnerable.

He'd been vulnerable with her and it was one of the most precious gifts he could have ever given her. He'd allowed himself to be defenseless, because he cared enough about her to want to stay, because he wanted to be with her more than he was afraid not to be.

Winnie got back into her car and released a shaky breath as she looked at Adam's sign. Tonight had been a dozen years in the making.

And she never imagined she'd have so much riding on the outcome.

# *13*

As Winnie's fingers threaded through his, Adam wheeled her car—she'd insisted that he drive, that it was an important part of her fantasy—onto the little dirt road that officially led to McKinney Point. His eyes widened when the headlights swung onto a familiar piece of scenery.

"You didn't," he said, stunned. "You painted another sign?"

Winnie grinned. "Not another sign. That's the sign."

He pulled into the space and cut his eyes to her. "The sign? You mean the same one?"

"One in the same."

He gave his head a bewildered shake. "You kept it?"

Winnie tuned the radio into a soft rock station and turned it down low. "Of course," she said, as though that were completely reasonable. "I put a lot of work into that sign and a lot of hours wondering who you were parked in front of it with," she told him. "I couldn't just throw it away. It had too much history."

He grunted. "Another sign is starting to make sense," he said, still stunned.

She frowned and popped two buttons on the front of her shirt, momentarily distracting him with her cleavage. "What sign?"

"The one above your back door."

She chuckled and crawled over into his lap, straddling him. "You mean 'I like my crazy'?" She kissed the corner of his mouth, wiggled sensuously against him. "I do, as it happens."

He couldn't keep up, not when she was on him like this. Kissing him, rubbing against him, making him hot. "What?"

She smiled against his lips. "Doesn't matter. I thought we were here to make out. Did you talk with all those other girls?"

Adam framed her face with his hands, angled her head and deepened the kiss. "I don't remember any other girls."

Winnie smiled against his lips. "Ooo. Right answer."

And then she was everywhere. Tugging at his shirt, slipping her small hand into his pants. Her fingers slid around him and tugged expertly bringing him perilously close to ending this make-out session before it ever really began. He slid his hands down her back, then up over her thighs beneath her skirt and gasped when he found nothing but bare flesh beneath.

"No panties?"

"I didn't think I was going to need them," she said, lifting him out of his shorts. Adam scooted the seat back, lowered it a bit, then managed to get his shorts out of the way enough to accommodate her impatient hands.

Two seconds later she was sinking onto him and his world narrowed into finer focus, one that only included her.

Winnie's mouth opened in a soft sigh of pleasure, as though her very life depended on this connection, as though nothing gave her more happiness than feeling him inside her.

The caveman urge to beat his chest threatened again and Adam prevented it by loosening the rest of her buttons on the front of her shirt and popping the front clasp on her lacy bra. The fabric sagged, clinging to her pert nipples. The sight of those perfect orbs barely covered with the decadent see-through material made a low hiss of satisfaction rumble from his throat.

He nudged the bra aside and drew a pouting nipple into his mouth.

"I love it when you do that," Winnie confessed, lifting up and sinking onto him once more. "I feel it here," she said, tightening around him and rocking forward."

He thumbed the other nipple, lest it feel neglected

and suckled harder, aroused by her candor. She made another little mewl of pleasure, rode him harder, tightened again and again squeezing, tugging, her sweet little body slowly but surely pushing him toward the point of no return.

Winnie took his head in her hands once more, dragging him away from her breasts and kissed him, leaning him further back against the seat. She tangled her tongue around his, sucked him deep into her mouth, then sampled the smooth flesh of his bottom lip. With every skilled swipe of her tongue, every mimicking movement of sex with their mouths, she rode him harder.

He shaped his hands around her ass, urging her on. Winnie wrapped her hands around the back of the headrest, holding on but effectively trapping him, and slid up and down his dick until he was certain that his balls were going to burst or he was going to die. Frankly, neither scenario mattered to him so long as she kept doing it.

Adam bucked wildly beneath her, desperately meeting her thrust for thrust, he shaped his hands over her ass, then wrapped them tightly around her waist and pounded into her, pushed harder and deeper, pistoning in and out of her with every bit of strength he possessed.

Winnie's breasts bounced on her chest, absorbing

his frenzied thrusts and her sweet nipples raked against his own.

It was desperate and frantic and sweet and all-consuming and he never wanted it to end, but couldn't wait to come. He'd surely die if he didn't.

Come into me, she'd said, the most erotic invitation he'd ever heard.

This was the last time he'd ever come into her, Adam thought and the idea made him all the more possessed. He pushed into her again, angling higher and he felt her convulse around him, heralding his own impending release.

Winnie's hands were back on his face, her thumbs sliding gently over his cheeks in a gesture that almost made him lose complete control because it was so heartfelt and tender in the midst of the most desperately depraved sex he'd ever had. Tender and frantic, mindless and raw.

His heart gave a little jolt and with a rush of emotion so sweet and so pure, Adam finally realized why this time with her was so special, so perfect, so beyond the scope of his imagination.

Because he loved her.

He'd known it, of course, but he'd never had the courage to admit it to himself. If he didn't admit it, then he could ignore it.

But the emotion battering against his heart, being

driven home by every undulation of her hips would not be denied.

He loved her.

Which was going to make leaving all the more difficult.

The thought was no sooner recognized than abandoned as Winnie suddenly spasmed around him, her hot little body rhythmically tightening against his own.

She kissed him again, deeply, and he came.

Hard.

The orgasm burst from his loins, bathing the back of her channel and her own release continued to pulse around him, sending little aftershocks of pleasure through him.

Breathing hard, Winnie drew back and kissed each of his eyelids, the tip of his nose, the soft patch of skin beneath his right eye, and then ultimately his mouth. Every brush her lips rang with the word neither of them wanted to face.

Goodbye.

Adam rested his forehead against hers, wishing things could be different, that he could be different. The truth that he'd been avoiding for months, the inescapable certainty of his own reality suddenly bore down on him, blasting through all of his carefully constructed defenses. He'd been tamping down his feelings for months, skirting around them in his own mind, refusing to fully acknowledge what he'd been ultimately afraid of because if he didn't dwell on it, if he merely knew it but didn't think about it, then maybe it wouldn't be true. Maybe it wouldn't be real.

He couldn't have her because he was damaged goods, Adam realized.

Broken.

Adam could never remember a time when he doubted himself. He'd always been confident in his abilities, never questioned his limits and never entertained the idea that he couldn't do something. "Can't" had never been a part of his vocabulary.

He never tried—he did.

Trying was a noble effort, but doing accomplished something.

He was more of a doer.

Unfortunately, that inherent unshakable confidence he'd always taken for granted had been blown all to hell and back right along with his leg, he realized now. He'd been trying for months to pull both back together again—pretending, even, that he had—but was finally ready to admit that his life was never going to be the same. It couldn't be.

Because he was different.

And with those differences came limitations. His future, regardless of what he tried to tell himself, was going to be different. But with that admission came a cache of other truths, ones he didn't want to claim, but had to deal with anyway.

Unfortunately, damn it all to hell, he had to deal with them now.

Adam had known from the instant that he'd awoken from surgery that his life was never going to be the same, had even considered the ways that it would be different. But knowing it—even peripherally—and truly grasping the concept were two completely different things.

He swallowed hard and passed a hand over his face, preparing to face the unhappy truth that had been haunting him from day one, the miserable fact that he'd never feel secure enough in his own body to ever marry or have children. To have any sort of life outside his career. And he'd almost blown that, as well.

Would he have minded so much if he hadn't realized that he wanted Winnie? Adam wondered. Would he have mourned the way he was grieving now for that lost future? Would the idea of her continuing her life with someone else—an image of a smirking Mark Holbrook loomed large in his mind and he mentally removed the self-satisfied smile with a strategic right hook—be so unbearable?

Honestly, who knew?

He only knew that he'd never inflict his disability

on anyone else—it wasn't fair—and most particularly on someone as vibrant and active as his Winnie.

His Winnie.

DID HE BELIEVE THAT he could ultimately have his career back? Yes. He was a damned fine soldier and he knew it. He was absolutely certain that when he walked into Colonel Marks' office tomorrow he would walk out with orders to return to Iraq.

But what he couldn't have—what he suddenly realized he wanted more than his next breath—was a real life with Winnie.

But if wishes were horses, then beggers would ride. And he didn't plan to be the begger in this relationship.

ADAM CAREFULLY STEERED Winnie's car into his parents' drive, shifted into park and killed the engine. Though she'd known this moment was coming, Winnie nevertheless wasn't prepared to face it.

She hadn't truly expected Adam to come to his senses tonight, to change his mind, but that didn't make their parting any less painful. Furthermore, though she didn't know what had gone on in that brilliant mind of his, Adam had changed tonight. The weariness she'd noted before was more pronounced and there was a shadow of sadness around him that he didn't seem to be able to shake. She wanted to comfort him, to help him, but she wasn't exactly sure how. For whatever reason, she got the impression that the demons he'd been running from had finally caught up with him.

Winnie cleared her throat and tried to find the words she needed to get through his final few minutes. "Thank you," she said, her voice sounding a bit strangled to her own ears. "I know you probably think it's silly, but you made more than a decade of dreaming come true tonight."

And he had. It had been purely magical, an evening she would never forget. Aside from the wonderful, frantic, poignant sex they'd had, they'd sat on the hood of her car, leaned against the windshield, stared out over the ocean and talked for hours. Books and movies, likes and dislikes, quirks and foibles, they'd shared it all. Done anything they could to prolong the evening, to avoid this very scenario.

Though Winnie had originally planned to make this very difficult for him, when push came to shove, she simply didn't have the heart. Adam was about to go back to war—to living hell on earth, by all accounts—and she would not, even though she selfishly wanted him for herself, do anything that was going to make that journey the least bit more difficult for him.

She couldn't.

Yes, she was a fighter, but this was a battle that

could wait for another time. She wasn't giving up—
she would never give up. She was merely retreating
for his own good.

He cleared his throat. "You don't have to thank me,
Winnie. It was my pleasure." The softest smile played
over his wickedly sensual mouth. "Quite literally."

She chuckled, despite herself. "What time do you
leave in the morning?"

"Six," he said. "The Colonel likes to beat the traffic."

She inclined her head. "Can I ask you something, Adam?"

He looked away, but not before she glimpsed the
self-loathing beginning in his eyes. She ached to
comfort him, to say anything that would make him
understand. But at this point, she had no idea what
combination of words would do just that. This was
something Adam was going to have to realize on his
own, in his own time, in his own way.

As for time…she had plenty of it.

"Are you even the least little bit afraid? Of going
back, I mean?"

He blinked, as though that wasn't the question
he'd been expecting. His expression cleared and he
studied her for a moment, his gaze searching hers.
"Yes," he said. "It's war. I'd be a fool if I wasn't a
little bit afraid." He leaned closer and the intensity,
the passion behind his eyes punched into her. "But

it's what I was born to do, Winnie. I'm a soldier. I've always been a soldier." He looked away. "I don't know how to be anything else."

She swallowed. The desperation in his voice cut her to the quick. Made her ache to soothe him. "So you'll return to your unit, to your former position?"

"I think so. I'll have to take extra precautions, but otherwise I don't think this—" He smacked his leg. "—is going to make any difference at all, you know?" He shook his head. "I could be fooling myself, but I don't think so."

She smiled and shot him an indulgent look. "Adam McPherson, there has never been a single thing in your life that you have not been able to achieve when you've set your mind to it. You're not fooling yourself." She nodded at him. "You're ready."

"Thanks to you," he said. Adam swallowed. "I owe it all to you."

"Nah, you just needed a little kick in the ass." She shrugged. "I'm always good for that."

"Seriously, Winnie, thank you." His fervent gaze bored into hers. "I don't know what I would have done these past couple of weeks without you. I'd like to think that I'd have crawled out of my room eventually, but…I don't know." He shook his head and drummed his thumb absently against the steering wheel. "I got stuck in my head and couldn't find my way out."

She swallowed and her throat tightened. "You'd been through a lot and hadn't had a moment to yourself to think. You were entitled to a bit of a funk," she said. "But when you looked like you might not snap out of it, I'll admit I had to act." She laughed, remembering. "You sure as hell didn't make it easy. I don't know exactly what it is you do in your job, but if it involves evading the enemy, then I'll bet you're damned good at it."

He chuckled and shook his head. "You're close. I'm a strategist. I plan our tactics, review exit strategies, and make contingency plans for every scenario."

She nodded, impressed. "Then I have every confidence that things will go the way you want them to in the morning." She looked at the clock on the dashboard. "Or rather this morning." Her eyes widened. "I didn't realize it was so late. Sorry."

He waved off her concern. "Time doesn't seem to matter when I'm with you."

Her gaze tangled with his at the unexpected compliment. "I, uh… I know that feeling, as well."

She was nearing the breaking point, Winnie thought. She couldn't hold it together much longer. If she wanted to finish this with any mascara left on at all and the slightest bit of her pride in tact, then she really needed to leave.

She started to open the passenger-side door. "I should probably—"

"Wait," he said, stopping her with a simple touch to her arm. His fingers were warm and calloused and she remembered them sliding over her body, testing every bit of her skin against his own. She closed her eyes and summoned the willpower to face him again.

"Don't you think—"

"I've got something for you," he said. He snagged a small package from beneath her front seat.

Her eyes widened. "How did that get there?"

He grinned. "I stashed it when you weren't looking."

Winnie shook her head. "Adam, I—"

He stayed her lips with another finger. "When a man offers you a gift, the polite thing to do is to accept it and say thank you."

Winnie blinked. She took the little present from his hand and dutifully did as he instructed. "Thank you."

He tsked and shook his head, as though she was a sad case. "You need to open it before saying thank you. Otherwise you don't know what you're thanking me for."

She didn't want to open it. She had a terrible feeling about this, one she couldn't explain. In any other circumstances she would have been thrilled to get a gift from Adam, but tonight? Tonight it didn't feel right. It felt too much like an official I'm-not-changing-my-mind goodbye.

"Go on," he encouraged. "Open it."

Hands trembling, Winnie reluctantly did as he asked. The gold paper came away quickly, revealing a small white box with Natalie's store logo on the top.

She looked at him and quirked a brow, intrigued. "You've been by the gallery?"

He rolled his eyes and gave an impatient huff. "Open the bloody box, Winnie. Please."

Winnie lifted the lid and a soft oomph of pleasure left her lips as she spied the little charm inside. She recognized it, of course—it was a slightly different replica of his. Different because no two pieces of driftwood were ever the same. But this was clearly the Chinese symbol for courage, the same as he wore himself.

Another little warning sounded in her mind, but she couldn't understand why, anymore than she could comprehend the sentiment behind the gift. Courage? What did she need courage for?

And then it hit her.

The courage to live her life without him. To move on. To find someone else.

Tears burned the backs of her eyes and she sincerely hoped that he would think they were tears of joy.

They were not.

He'd ruined her again, laid waste to her heart, the one he seemed absolutely determined to reject from now on.

She struggled to say something appropriate. "Wow. Th-thank you." She cleared her throat. "It's like yours."

His eyes were kind, but determined. "I know."

"Would you like to explain why you chose this particular charm?" she asked, a glutton for punishment.

Adam looked away and she was thankful that he appeared to be struggling, that his mouth didn't want to form the words his mind had determined were necessary. "I chose it because I want you to have the courage to find another life, Winnie. One without me in it. You've got to promise me that you'll do it," he said. "I can't go off thinking that you're waiting, that you're expecting—" He broke off, unable to continue. "I need to let go, Winnie."

A fatalistic smile rolled around her lips and the tears she'd been determined that she wasn't going to cry spilled over.

So she'd been right.

And naturally he'd ask the one thing of her she wasn't able to give.

Asking her not to love him, not to want him, not to miss him was like asking her not to breathe.

It was impossible.

Winnie shook her head and her blurry gaze tangled with his. She tightened her fist around the little charm, because she needed the courage right then to say what had to be said.

"I'm sorry, Adam, but that's a promise I can't make. Because, as you and everyone else in town knows, I love you." She laughed brokenly, the relief at admitting it aloud making her slightly manic. "I have always loved you. I will always love you. I can't just turn it off, like there's a button somewhere. If that were the case, then I would have done it a long time ago, especially when you didn't seem to realize that I existed."

"Winnie, I never—"

She jumped out the car, rounded the hood and opened the driver's side door, silently asking him to get out. He did, but very reluctantly. Always a gentleman, she thought. He didn't turn that off, either.

"Winnie—"

"Save it, Adam. And you can keep your charm." She handed it back to him, then slid behind the wheel and closed the door. She looked at him through the open window, though it hurt. "I'm not the one who needs courage. That's you. You're the coward here. You're afraid to let yourself love me."

"I'm not afraid, dammit. It's impossible. I can't have that dream anymore. I'm not—"

"Bullshit. Just like everything else in your life, Adam, you could have it if you wanted it bad enough, if it were truly important to you."

His temper flared. "Don't tell me you're not important to me! Don't tell me I don't want it enough. You have no idea," he said, emphasizing ever word.

"Maybe not," she said, shrugging. "But talk is cheap and your reasoning is flawed. If you can have your career back, then you can have it all back. You can have me back. If you wanted me."

She started the car.

"Winnie, wait! You don't understand—" He swore hotly. "Dammit, I'm botching this."

"What do you want from me, Adam?" she all but wailed. She could feel tears burning the backs of her eyes and determinedly blinked them back. "I'm tired of trying to figure you out. I'm weary of your games. Why can't you just level with me? Why can't you just tell me the damned truth? All of it, in plain English, not veiled in innuendo and cryptic meaning. Please," she tacked on as an afterthought. Her voice broke with despair.

His agonized eyes tangled with hers and the swirl of emotion she saw churning there made her ache to comfort him. But she couldn't. Not anymore. If he wanted her comfort, then he was going to have to ask for it, dammit. She was through. She couldn't do this anymore. She didn't have the strength.

"I'm not good enough for you anymore!" he finally exploded, as though the words had been ripped from a hidden, hated part of himself, a part he kept tightly under rein. "Not like this! Look at me," he said, disgust dripping from his voice. He gestured wearily to his missing leg. "I can't keep up with you. I can't even run without friggin' falling down. I'm a wreck, Winnie. A house condemned. Can't you see that?"

So she'd had it right, then. But he was far worse than she'd feared. His admission left her reeling, the revulsion for himself the most terrible part in all of this. Her beautiful wounded warrior. He was wrong on so many counts she didn't even know where to begin.

"I won't do this to you," he said, shaking his head. Determination rang in his tone. "I won't drag you into it. And I'm not going to take advantage of your…affection—"

He'd meant to say love—he knew she loved him.

"—because I can't distinguish between it and pity. It's not fair to you."

"Let's leave how I feel about you out of it for a minute please. How do you feel about me?"

He hesitated. "Winnie—"

She squeezed her eyes tightly shut, then opened them once more. "Tell me."

He swallowed and though it could only be her imagination playing tricks on her, she thought he looked…nervous. She'd never seen Adam McPherson nervous about anything.

He cleared his throat. "I…care very…deeply for you. But that doesn't change anything. Don't put your hope in me, Winnie," he said, his voice breaking. "I'm hopeless."

"No, you're not," she said fervently. She reached out and grabbed his hand. "I don't ever want to hear you say that again."

He laughed without humor. "It's true."

"It's not," she insisted. "Let me ask you something, Adam. You're determined to get your career back, right? To go back to Iraq? Resume your Special Forces position?"

He nodded.

"So you can have your career back, but the rest of your life is lost to you? You can't have me?"

"In a manner of speaking, yes."

Outraged at his skewed reasoning, Winnie felt her eyes widen. "That's flawed logic, genius. Surely you see it?"

A shadow moved behind his eyes. "Flawed or not, it's mine. I won't hurt you, Winnie."

Wrong, Winnie thought. What did he think he was doing to her now?

She smiled sadly. "All the same, Adam, I'm here. Just like always. You can't change how I feel anymore than I can. You can't make me not want you. You can't make me not love you. You can't make me not want a life with you." She looked away, unable to stand the pain on his face, the indecision. "And I will never stop wanting that or trying to make you want it, too." She swallowed, knowing truer words had never been spoken. He was hers, dammit. She knew he loved her. She would win…in time. "Be safe."

And with those two words, she shifted into Reverse and drove away from him.

It was the hardest thing she'd ever done in her life.

# _14_

COLONEL MARKS STOOD and shook his hand. "Congratulations, Captain McPherson. It's a pleasure to have you back with us."

Adam smiled, though the victory he'd expected to feel rang hollowly. "Thank you, sir. My pleasure."

"You're sure Monday isn't too soon? You're ready?"

"Absolutely," Adam said, tasting the barest hint of a lie on his tongue. He was ready to go back to Iraq, but he was not ready to leave Winnie.

_I'm here, Adam, just like always…_

Sweet hell, did she have any idea what she was doing to him? How much he wanted to believe that she was right and they could have it all?

"I know we've added some unexpected duties to your actual job description, but I hope that they will be something that will be both rewarding to you and to your fellow injured brothers in arms."

Adam nodded once. "Yes, sir. It'll be an honor."

And it would, though he really didn't feel like he

had any business telling other wounded soldiers how to recover when he was far from recovered himself. His little revelations last night had told him just how far he still had to go. Physically, yes he was ready to go back to work. But mentally… Like he'd told Winnie last night, he was a wreck. A house condemned. Uninhabitable.

As for the additional duties, Adam knew there were other amputees who shared their stories to instill hope, to show the wounded that, while their lives and bodies might be broken, they were not shattered beyond repair. Though he had his doubts, what Colonel Marks had asked him specifically to do really appealed to him. The idea of helping other men and women who wanted re-entry into their former positions, teaching them how to meet that goal was intensely appealing.

While he wasn't altogether sure he knew exactly what he was doing, he knew how not to do it. And he knew what these people were going through. He could relate. He could inspire. He could still lead.

Curiously, this new purpose sparked a surge of adrenaline he hadn't felt in a long time, could sense the thrill of a new purpose, a new direction cutting a path across his future. Strange when he'd been so certain his path had been set, that there'd never be another road he wanted to follow…

He exited the building and found his parents sitting on a bench beneath a wide oak tree.

"Well?" his father asked.

Adam smiled and nodded once. "I'm back."

His father grinned, gripped him in a hug and slapped him on the back. "Well done, son. I'm proud of you."

His mother's arms came around his waist. "And despite what you think, I am too."

"Mom," he said chidingly.

"No, it's true. I am proud of you. If this is truly the life you want, then I'm happy for you, too."

Until last night Adam would have whole-heartedly agreed that this was indeed the life he wanted. Actually, that wasn't true. It was still the life he wanted…he just wanted Winnie to share it with him.

That's why the victory felt hollow—because she wasn't here to share it with him. He wanted to tell her how everything had gone, tell her about his new mentoring opportunity, one that Colonel Marks intimated might actually turn into a full-time position based here in the States, where he would split time between Walter Reed Medical Center and The Center for the Intrepid.

That would be after he finished his tour, of course, but technically his tour was up in two months. While this wasn't strictly getting his old job back, Adam felt like this path had opened for a reason and it didn't feel wrong.

"You should call Winnie and let her know," his mother said. "She'll be so pleased for you."

She would be, Adam thought. Winnie would be happy about anything that made him happy. Because she loved him. He laughed softly. Because she'd always loved him.

Adam mentally reviewed their last few minutes together and marveled at her tenacity, at her determination. His little fighter, he thought, smiling.

And he'd had the nerve to give her a courage charm?

Winnie was right. She wasn't the one who needed courage—he was.

Because he'd been afraid to love her, afraid of the future, afraid of becoming a burden. But he'd just realized something very important, something that shifted his reasoning and made a mockery of his so-called logic.

He was more afraid of living without her.

For all intents and purposes, the comprehension was so strong the ground should have shook beneath his feet.

It was true that in all probability at some point in their future, he would not be able to keep up with Winnie. He still believed that. He would treat his body well, he would show it the kindness it needed to continue healing. But at some point, he would start to fade. When he did, the difficulties that came with old age were going to be exacerbated by the fact he was an amputee.

This was not speculation—this was fact.

But that was his hang-up, not Winnie's.

And it was not worth squandering the rest of their lives, their very futures and possible children over.

Furthermore, while Winnie might love her little bakery and her niche in Bethel Bay...she loved him more. She would follow him wherever he might go and always be glad to be there. He knew this, not because she'd told him, but because she didn't have to.

Winnie Cuthbert, against better sense, for whatever reason, genuinely truly loved him...and she didn't care that he was damaged.

Could a man get anymore lucky?

Could a man be anymore stupid for trying to throw that away?

No.

Adam McPherson was many things, but stupid was not among them.

"We should probably get going, son," his father said. "Where do we need to take your things?"

Adam looked up at his father. "Back to Bethel Bay for the weekend, General."

A look of surprise crossed his father's face. "With us? But I thought you said you were staying here."

"Change of plans. I've got to right a wrong before I leave."

"But you're leaving Monday?"

"Yessir, that's when I ship out. But don't worry about having to drive me back up here," he said, smiling as a plan fully solidified in his mind. Happiness burst through him, washing away any sense of doubt, any inkling of uneasiness. "With luck, my wife will do that."

His mother gasped with pleasure and she lifted her fingers to her mouth to hide her overwhelmingly wide smile. "Tell Winnie I said hello."

Adam nodded, suddenly energized with purpose, absolutely desperate to get back to her. "I always do."

WINNIE STARED AT the chocolate cupcake she'd just iced and blinked back tears.

Stupid cupcake.

Instead of working the counter like she normally did, she'd hid in the kitchen the better part of the morning so that she could be alone. Lizzie and Jeanette knew that something was wrong. They'd probably also guessed that something's name and were thankfully, blessedly, leaving her alone.

She preferred to nurse her wounds in private.

She deliberately licked the chocolate icing off the cupcake she'd just covered.

She was pathetic.

She'd known this was coming. And yet none of that prepared her for the yawning emptiness in her life that Adam's absence had left.

She set her tools aside and curled her arms around her middle, trying with every bit of willpower she had left to hold the pieces of her heart together.

It couldn't be broken beyond repair because it still beat. She knew at some point she would recover.

But she would still love him.

Had he gotten his position back? Winnie wondered. Was he as happy as he expected to be? Was he eager to return to his unit? To finish the tour of duty he started? These are all things she'd love to ask him, ached to ask him, but was no longer welcome to do so.

Winnie hung her head and tried to find some enthusiasm for her work, but failed miserably. Unfortunately, while she'd been off for the past couple of days, she'd gotten behind on her baking and had no choice but to play catch up now. It was bake or starve, Winnie thought, and the idea drew a weary smile over her lips. And she still had play-offs to get ready for. There was nothing like some good stiff competition to get her mind off her troubles.

"Winnie?" Jeanette called. "There's someone out here who wants to see you."

Dammit, she'd asked them to handle things up front today, that she wasn't fit company for customers. She'd managed to make it most of the morning and afternoon huddled back in her kitchen. Was a few more minutes too much to ask?

"I've got my hands in something, Jeanette, and can't walk away. Could you please help them with whatever it is?"

She heard Jeanette snicker. "Er…I don't think so."

"Liar," she heard a woefully familiar voice say from the kitchen doorway.

Winnie gasped and whirled around.

Adam.

But he was gone— He left this morning— He wasn't supposed to be back— How—

"If a cupcake is the only thing standing between me and a private audience with you, then by all means let me help you." He sidled forward and snagged the mangled cupcake from her hand and popped the rest of it into his mouth. He swallowed. "See how easy that was. Now you're free, right?"

Winnie blinked, astounded. "W-what are you doing here," she asked faintly. She gripped the metal table, not altogether sure that her wobbly knees were going to support her.

He smiled, and the insecurity she'd seen in previous grins was nowhere to be seen. This was Adam's smile, the confident, self-assured I-know-what-I-want-and-I'm-getting-it-come-hell-or-high-water grin.

Hope inexplicably blossomed in her chest and her breathing sped up.

He withdrew a small velvet box from his pocket and showed it to her. "It occurred to me today that I'd given you the wrong piece of jewelry last night."

Her heart threatened to pound out of her chest and for the first time in her life, she was in danger of hyperventilating. "W-wrong piece of j-jewelry?" she repeated.

He nodded solemnly, dropped to his knee and opened the box. A single solitaire blinked from the satiny folds. Or at least that's what she thought she saw. It was hard to tell with a sheen of tears blocking her view.

"Adam," she choked out.

"Winnie, I love you," he said, his voice sure and emphatic. "You were right when you called me a coward. I've been afraid. I'm still a bit of a mess and I come with a lot of hangups, but…I'm more afraid of a future without you. I need you." He swallowed. "Will you marry me?"

She sank to her knees, as well, her bottom lip between her teeth. Shaking all over, she merely nodded.

"Today?"

She blinked, stunned. "Today?"

Another grin. "I ship out on Monday."

"Oh."

"And I don't want to do it without making you mine. I know that I'm asking you to give up a wedding and cake and guests and gifts and—"

She threw her arms around his neck, then pressed her lips in her favorite spot beneath his ear and breathed him in. "Do you think any of that matters to me, you fool? I get you. I win."

He chuckled against her. "You might not think I'm such a prize after we're married. I hear that happens."

Winnie drew back and looked at him through her tears. Those bright sea eyes were alight with happiness and triumph. The idea that he loved her, that he wanted her forever spilled into every cell in her body, making her rejoice with utter contentment.

"I win," she repeated. "And you have always been and will always be my prize."

His gaze softened and he bent forward and kissed her. "You're too good for me."

"I know," she teased. "But why let a little thing like that keep us apart?"

Adam grinned. "Why, indeed."

# *Epilogue*

*Two months later...*

BECAUSE HE KNEW BETTER than to expect that his wife would be home, Adam went immediately to the bakery and dropped his duffel bag onto the floor.

Jeanette squealed with delight and Lizzie whooped for joy. "You're back early! Winnie didn't say—"

"She doesn't know." This was supposed to be a surprise. He glanced around, peered into the kitchen and frowned when he didn't see her. "Where is she?"

Jeanette and Lizzie shared a look.

"What?" he asked, growing alarmed.

"She's in the bathroom," Lizzie said, but there was something in her tone that gave Adam pause.

He frowned. "Is she sick?"

Their lips quivered. "Nothing she won't get over in a couple of months."

Still worried and puzzled over their enigmatic behavior, Adam strolled into the hall and waited patiently for Winnie to come out of the bathroom. He heard an ominous noise, one he recognized and worry descended on him. She was sick? Throwing up? A moment later, the toilet flushed, then the faucet ran and he detected the unmistakable sound of her brushing her teeth.

After what felt like an eternity, his wife—his wife, he thought, amazed at how proud that made him feel—opened the door and stepped into the narrow hall. She gasped and squealed when she saw him, then launched herself into his arms.

"Adam! What are you doing here? I thought you weren't getting in until tomorrow. I was going to come and get you," she chided softly.

"I caught an earlier flight," he told her, feeling the peace of finally being with her again wash through him, settle around him, anchor him home once more. He drew back. "Are you okay? It sounded like you were sick in there."

She blinked, then a small secret smile slid over her lips. "I'm completely fine. In fact, I've never been better."

He didn't understand. He knew she'd just thrown up. He'd heard her.

"Actually, I need to amend that statement. We've never been better."

Adam felt his heart skip a beat as he quickly put

the odd behavior, her sudden malaise and the euphoric look on Winnie's face together in his mind to form the most logical answer. "We?"

She nodded once, her face alight with joy. "Yes, our twins and I."

Adam felt his eyes widen and joy bolted through him. "Twins? You're sure?"

She smiled. "Turns out I wasn't as protected as I thought I was. My birth control failed. I went to the doctor when I didn't start and he did an ultrasound to confirm."

"Twins," Adam breathed. He shook his head. "You know, I didn't think that I could be any happier than when I just saw you…but I am."

Winnie smiled. "So where are we going next?" she asked. "New orders yet?"

Ah. His good news. And it was good news. While he would have never chosen this new opportunity in the past, he couldn't imagine his life taking a different direction now. He was still a soldier the same as he'd always been, but he had a different purpose now, one that he was even more passionate about. Granted there were many things about his new life he didn't fully understand—and he still had a few kinks in his head—but he could help people. He'd lived their nightmare and could relate. In short, he could help.

"Nowhere," he told her, smiling. "How would you

feel if I told you I'd been offered that mobile position I'd told you about?"

She gasped. "The mentoring opportunity? You'd be able to commute?"

He nodded. "The longest I would ever be away is two weeks at a stretch."

Her eyes lit up and a slow smile dawned over her unbelievably beautiful mouth. She snorted. "Two weeks is a walk in the park compared to the last two months. I've missed you."

He hugged her tightly. "I've missed you, too."

Winnie drew back. "Are you sure about this, Adam? We'll do whatever makes you happy, because I'm happy where you are."

He knew that and he appreciated it. But he was certain. He'd proved to himself that he hadn't lost anything, absolutely nothing at all. In fact, he'd gained everything his heart ever desired.

"I'm sure," he said. He nuzzled her neck. "You know what I've been craving?"

"A cupcake?"

"Hmm. That, too, but it can wait. I've actually been having the oddest craving for…powdered sugar. Think you can hook me up?"

Winnie leaped up and wrapped her legs around his waist. Her sexy mouth found his and her arms tightened possessively around his neck, making him feel more complete than he ever had in his life. Desire burned through his blood, pooled in his groin and caught fire.

"I've got your fix," she breathed against his lips.

And she did.

\* \* \* \* \*

*Celebrate 60 years of pure reading pleasure with Harlequin!*

To commemorate the event, Harlequin Intrigue® is thrilled to invite you to the wedding of The Colby Agency's J. T. Baxley and his bride, Eve Mattson.

That is, of course, if J.T. can find the woman who left him at the altar. Considering he's a private investigator for one of the top agencies in the country—the best of the best—that shouldn't be a problem. The real setback is that his bride isn't who she appears to be…and her mysterious past has put them both in danger.

*Enjoy an exclusive glimpse of Debra Webb's latest addition to*
THE COLBY AGENCY: ELITE RECONNAIS-SANCE DIVISION

*THE BRIDE'S SECRETS*

*Available August 2009 from Harlequin Intrigue®.*

The dark figures on the dock were still firing. The bullets cutting through the surface of the water without the warning boom of shots told Eve they were using silencers.

That was to her benefit. Silencers decreased the accuracy of every shot and lessened the range.

She grabbed for the rocks. Scrambled through the darkness. Bumped her knee on a boulder. Cursed.

Burrowing into the waist-deep grass, she kept low and crawled forward. Faster. Pushed harder. Needed as much distance as possible.

Shots pinged on the rocks.

J.T. scrambled alongside her.

He was breathing hard.

They had to stay close to the ground until they reached the next row of warehouses. Even though she was relatively certain they were out of range at this point, she wasn't taking any risks. And she wasn't slowing down.

J.T. had to keep up.

The splat of a bullet hitting the ground next to Eve had her rolling left. Maybe they weren't completely out of range.

She bumped J.T. He grunted.

His injured arm. Dammit. She could apologize later.

Half a dozen more yards.

Almost in the clear.

As she reached the cover of the alley between the first two warehouses she tensed.

Silence.

No pings or splats.

She glanced back at the dock. Deserted.

Time to run.

Her car was parked another block down.

Pushing to her feet, she sprinted forward. The wet bag dragged at her shoulder. She ignored it.

By the time she reached the lot where her car was parked, she had dug the keys from her pocket and hit the fob. Six seconds later she was behind the wheel. She hit the ignition as J.T. collapsed into the passenger seat. Tires squealed as she spun out of the slot.

"What the hell did you do to me?"

From the corner of her eye she watched him shake his head in an attempt to clear it.

He would be pissed when she told him about the tranquilizer.

She'd needed him cooperative until she formulated a plan. A drug-induced state of unconsciousness had been the fastest and most efficient method to ensure his continued solidarity.

"I can't really talk right now." Eve weaved into the right lane as the street widened to four lanes. What she needed was traffic. It was Saturday night—shouldn't be that difficult to find as soon as they were out of the old warehouse district.

A glance in the rearview mirror warned that their unwanted company had caught up.

Sensing her tension, J.T. turned to peer over his left shoulder.

"I hope you have a plan B."

She shot him a look. "There's always plan G." Then she pulled the Glock out of her waistband.

Cutting the steering wheel left, she slid between two vehicles. Another veer to the right and she'd put several cars between hers and the enemy.

She was betting they wouldn't pull out the firepower in the open like this, but a girl could never be too sure when it came to an unknown enemy.

Deep blending was the way to go.

Two traffic lights ahead the marquis of a movie theater provided exactly the opportunity she was looking for.

The digital numbers on the dash indicated it was

just past midnight. Perfect timing. The late movie would be purging its audience into the crowd of teenagers who liked hanging out in the parking lot.

She took a hard right onto the property that sported a twelve-screen theater, numerous fast-food hot spots and a chain superstore. Speeding across the lot, she selected a lane of parking slots. Pulling in as close to the theater entrance as possible, she shut off the engine and reached for her door.

"Let's go."

Thankfully he didn't argue.

Rounding the hood of her car, she shoved the Glock into her bag, then wrapped her arm around J.T.'s and merged into the crowd.

With her free hand she finger-combed her long hair. It was soaked, as were her clothes. The kids she bumped into noticed, gave her death-ray glares.

They just didn't know.

As she and J.T. moved in closer to the building, she grabbed a baseball cap from an innocent by-stander. The crowd made it easy. The kid who owned the cap had made it even easier by stuffing the cap bill-first into his waistband at the small of his back.

Pushing through the loitering crowd, she made her way to the side of the building next to the main entrance. She pushed J.T. against the wall and dropped her bag to the ground. Peeled off her tee and let it fall.

His gaze instantly zeroed in on her breasts, where the cami she wore had glued to her skin like an extra layer. A zing of desire shot through his veins.

Not the time.

With a flick of her wrist she twisted her hair up and clamped the cap atop the blonde mass.

"They're coming," J.T. muttered as he gazed at some point beyond her.

"Yeah, I know." She planted her palms against the wall on either side of him and leaned in. "Keep your eyes open. Let me know when they're inside."

Then she planted her lips on his.

\* \* \* \* \*

*Will J.T. and Eve be caught in the moment?*
*Or will Eve get the chance to reveal*
*all of her secrets?*
*Find out in*
***THE BRIDE'S SECRETS***
*by Debra Webb*
*Available August 2009 from Harlequin Intrigue®*

**We'll be spotlighting a different series every month throughout 2009 to celebrate our 60th anniversary.**

## LOOK FOR
## HARLEQUIN INTRIGUE®
## IN AUGUST!

To commemorate the event, Harlequin Intrigue® is thrilled to invite you to the wedding of the Colby Agency's J.T. Baxley and his bride, Eve Mattson.

**Look for *Colby Agency: Elite Reconnaissance***

# THE BRIDE'S SECRETS
## BY DEBRA WEBB

*Available August 2009*

**www.eHarlequin.com**

HIBPA09

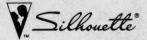
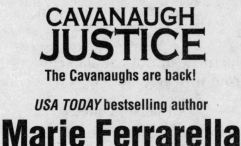

# Do you crave dark and sensual paranormal tales?

## Get your fix with Silhouette Nocturne!

### In print:
Two new titles available every month wherever books are sold.

### Online:
Nocturne eBooks available monthly from **www.silhouettenocturne.com.**

### Nocturne Bites:
Short sensual paranormal stories available monthly online from **www.nocturnebites.com** and in print with the Nocturne Bites collections available April 2009 and October 2009 wherever books are sold.

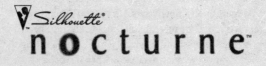

www.silhouettenocturne.com
www.paranormalromanceblog.com

SNBITESRG

**Stay up-to-date on all your romance reading news!**

The Inside Romance newsletter is a **FREE** quarterly newsletter highlighting our upcoming series releases and promotions!

**Go to eHarlequin.com/InsideRomance**

or e-mail us at
**InsideRomance@Harlequin.com**
to sign up to receive
your **FREE** newsletter today!

# REQUEST YOUR FREE BOOKS!

## 2 FREE NOVELS PLUS 2 FREE GIFTS!

HARLEQUIN®

*Blaze*™

**Red-hot reads!**

**YES!** Please send me 2 FREE Harlequin® Blaze™ novels and my 2 FREE gifts (gifts are worth about $10). After receiving them, if I don't wish to receive any more books, I can return the shipping statement marked "cancel." If I don't cancel, I will receive 6 brand-new novels every month and be billed just $4.24 per book in the U.S. or $4.71 per book in Canada. That's a savings of 15% off the cover price. It's quite a bargain. Shipping and handling is just 50¢ per book.* I understand that accepting the 2 free books and gifts places me under no obligation to buy anything. I can always return a shipment and cancel at any time. Even if I never buy another book, the two free books and gifts are mine to keep forever.

151 HDN EYS2   351 HDN EYTE

| | |
|---|---|
| Name | (PLEASE PRINT) |
| Address | Apt. # |
| City | State/Prov. | Zip/Postal Code |

Signature (if under 18, a parent or guardian must sign)

Mail to the **Harlequin Reader Service:**
**IN U.S.A.:** P.O. Box 1867, Buffalo, NY 14240-1867
**IN CANADA:** P.O. Box 609, Fort Erie, Ontario L2A 5X3

Not valid to current subscribers of Harlequin Blaze books.

**Want to try two free books from another line?**
**Call 1-800-873-8635 or visit www.morefreebooks.com.**

* Terms and prices subject to change without notice. Prices do not include applicable taxes. N.Y. residents add applicable sales tax. Canadian residents will be charged applicable provincial taxes and GST. Offer not valid in Quebec. This offer is limited to one order per household. All orders subject to approval. Credit or debit balances in a customer's account(s) may be offset by any other outstanding balance owed by or to the customer. Please allow 4 to 6 weeks for delivery. Offer available while quantities last.

**Your Privacy:** Harlequin Books is committed to protecting your privacy. Our Privacy Policy is available online at www.eHarlequin.com or upon request from the Reader Service. From time to time we make our lists of customers available to reputable third parties who may have a product or service of interest to you. If you would prefer we not share your name and address, please check here. ☐

HB09R3

# COMING NEXT MONTH

## Available July 28, 2009

### #483 UNBRIDLED  Tori Carrington
After being arrested for a crime he didn't commit, former Marine Carter Southard is staying far away from the one thing that's always gotten him into trouble—women! Unfortunately, his sexy new attorney, Laney Cartwright, is making that very difficult….

### #484 THE PERSONAL TOUCH  Lori Borrill
Professional matchmaker Margot Roth needs to give her latest client the personal touch—property mogul Clint Hilton is a playboy extraordinaire and is looking for a date…for his mother. But while Margot's setting up mom, Clint decides Margot's for him. Let the seduction begin!

### #485 HOT UNDER PRESSURE  Kathleen O'Reilly
*Where You Least Expect It*
Ashley Larsen and David McLean are hot for each other. Who knew the airport would be the perfect place to find the perfect sexual partner? But can the lust last when it's a transcontinental journey every time these two want to hook up?

### #486 SLIDING INTO HOME  Joanne Rock
*Encounters*
*Take me out to the ball game…* Four sexy major leaguers are duking it out for the ultimate prize—the Golden Glove award. Little do they guess that the women fate puts in their path will offer them even more of a challenge…and a much more satisfying reward!

### #487 STORM WATCH  Jill Shalvis
*Uniformly Hot!*
During his stint in the National Guard, Jason Mauer had seen his share of natural disasters. But when he finds himself in a flash flood with an old crush—sexy Lizzy Mann—the waves of desire turn out to be too much….

### #488 THE MIGHTY QUINNS: CALLUM  Kate Hoffmann
*Quinns Down Under*
Gemma Moynihan's sexy Irish eyes are smiling on Callum Quinn! Charming the ladies has never been quiet Cal's style. But he plans to charm the pants off luscious Gemma—until he finds out she's keeping a dangerous secret...

HBCNMBPA0709